T0046495

A CALABASH OF COWRIES

A Calabash of Cowries: Ancient Wisdom for Modern Times.
Copyright © 2023 by Luisah Teish. All rights reserved.
ISBN: 978-1-60801-247-3.

Cover image: Nedra Williams, *Queen Africa*. 2022.
Cover design by Alex Dimeff.

"Peace Nana" was originally published in *Peace Prayers: Meditations,
Affirmations, Invocations, Poems, and Prayers for Peace*, Harper San
Francisco, edited by Carrie Leadingham, Joann E. Moschella, and
Hilary M. Vartanian. 1992. ISBN 0-06-250464-9 Pgs 50-51.

"Mother of Night" was originally published in *The Shift Catalyst* issue
20, Oct 20, 2019, published by The Shift Network

Printed in the United States of America on acid-free paper.
First edition.

UNIVERSITY OF NEW ORLEANS PRESS
2000 Lakeshore Drive
New Orleans, Louisiana 70148
unopress.org

A CALABASH OF COWRIES

ancient wisdom for modern times

LUISAH TEISH

Dedication

Dedicated to my four Mothers:
Iyalode Oshun Ibukole, my Orisha mother
Serena Scott Allen, my biological mother
Moma Lola, my mambo mother in Voudoun
Iya OmiAladora, my Egungun mother

Libations/Invocation

Libations should always be poured for the ancestors.
Remember that water, juices, or alcohol can all be used.
Simply pour the liquid on the ground or the floor of the
altar four times and say:
"May my hands be fresh.
May the road be clear.
May the house be clean.
May the spirit of the ancestors be fresh."

CONTENTS

Part III: The Casting

Appendices

FOREWORD

A Calabash of Cowries: Ancient Wisdom for Modern Times by Yeye Luisah Teish is a book of stories. But these stories are not "just stories." They carry cultural weight and impart values. Their meanings and interpretations have significant effects on social behavior. They influence the social mores and legal decisions that govern daily lives, especially women's lives. As Teish says, "Women have struggled for decades to heal the mythology from its patriarchal wounding."

We have felt the soul impact of stories that subordinate, minimize, and degrade women, whether they are told in scriptures, songs, novels, or movies. This is why Teish and I went looking for other stories in the early 1970s. We looked beyond the dominant narratives of great men, of gods with women in their shadows.

Historians often talk about stratification, discerning the layers—in archaeology, in texts, in scriptures—that build up over time. Some ancient themes get buried; others carry through but are altered and revised, and certain stories are elevated over others. What prevails in the dominant narratives, all too often, are stories that elevate men and make women (goddesses) flawed or lacking. These revisions have a sociopolitical valence. Feminist researchers noticed how goddesses got changed into gods or had their importance reduced and whittled away. These patterns are visible in ancient Sumerian literature, some of the oldest texts in the world. We can trace them, too, in China, India, Greece, and Mexico, among other places.

So, it is important to sift back through the mythology for the goddesses who have been covered over or recast in negative forms. Teish has done this with the story of Obba in this volume, pointing out a key insight of women's historical recovery: look to the local; go to the roots. Obba is made to look foolish in the version of her story that has become predominant. But in talking to many elders, Teish found out that the version that has Obba cut off her own ear came from a single village—the others told it very differently (and you can read that alternate version in this book).

In this volume, Teish has brought forward stories that challenged the men-first, or men-only, protocols of patriarchal society. She emphasizes Oshun—without whom life could not flourish and all undertakings fail—in a story that rearranges assumptions about what female potency really is and how foundational it is to the world. Omit it, and you lose sight of truth, of reality.

Together we searched for the divine in female form, for the fullness, and began learning the names and forms of little-known goddesses. This took some digging, backgrounded and deprecated as they were, often cast as "the wife of [whatever male god]." We had to go down through the overlays, the footnotes, into the deep deposits, and there we found Neith, mother of the gods, "the primordial one, eldest of the primeval gods, She who made that which is, She who created that which exists." We found Nyame and Nana Buruku, Asherah and Anu and Nammu—a vast international litany of goddesses.[1]

---

1   See my *Creatrix Litany* on my YouTube channel.

I've spent over half a century attempting to reconstruct women's history and heritage from a global perspective. As I examine the cultural record—not just the dynastic histories or religious canons, but the archaeology, the iconography, the orature—I see recurring patterns: the deep layers of matricultural themes—the motherpots, the female figurines in their ceremonial paint-up and regalia, the women's dances—subsumed by the advent of authoritarian rulership upheld by warfare and patriarchal social hierarchy. Our search for the mythology of liberation continues today.

Calabash reexamines the spiritual-cultural myths of the African diaspora. It liberates indigenous orature from the cultural racism of the colonial period. Scholars of the diaspora recognize that orature carries the essence of the tradition. It is not a written tradition; it is living, breathing—literally transmitted through the breath. This is where Yeye Luisah Teish excels, as a storyteller who expounds the teachings in her deep, rich voice; who imparts meanings, understands implications, and, in the process, recreates living culture. Teish is a gifted oral storyteller, using her dramatic talents to great effect—and the woman can write, expertly drawing on a treasure house of cultural metaphors and melodic texture.

The reclamation and restoration of ancestral wisdom and ceremony have been at the heart of her work for more than half a century. It is cherished by an international stellium of communities who call her Yeye and respect her foundational work at the crucial juncture of African spirituality and the liberatory passion of women.

One of the many African American women who have been inspired by Teish is Dr. Teresa N. Washington, author of *Our Mothers, Our Powers, Our Texts: Manifestation of* Àjé *in Africana Literature* (2005). She writes in the introduction, "Spiritualist Luisah Teish gave me a reading and some soul food with [her book] *Jambalaya*," and she alludes to Teish's work elsewhere in the text. What Washington says of Zora Neale Hurston, the forerunner of this spiritual reclamation, applies to Teish as well: "She knew that there was something deeper, larger—there was a Yewájobì—a Mother of all Òrìsà (gods) and life forms. Her name is disremembered, but Her visage is only a clear lake away."[2]

Luisah Teish comes bringing the stories, seeking out and liberating teachings of the goddesses and how their powers move in people's lives. She comes clothed in the colors and ornaments of Oshun, waving her fan to clear the cultural air of harmful prejudices and negativities. She carries the clear, cooling water that heals and restores, and she pours it out in the name of the Orishas. She is a culture bearer who brings forth new recitations of the ancient stories, jewels out of the West African and African American heritage. She has stood like an iroko[3] and said: "Here are the taproots; let us draw up from the deep."

Yeye Teish is a drum for Oshun, resounding truths through her storytelling.

Max Dashu
Founder, Suppressed Histories Archives

---

2   Published by Oya's Tornado (2015): p. 5.
3   A large hardwood tree that grows in West Africa and is known to live up to five hundred years. It is used to carve sacred stools, statues, and masks. Reputed to have healing properties.

INTRODUCTION

A Calabash of Cowries: Ancient Wisdom for Modern Times is a book of myths, legends, and folktales that describe the wonders of the natural world, the adventures of illustrious ancestors, and the powers of the Orishas,[4] the primary archetypes of the African diaspora.

The African diaspora, which originates in West and Central Africa, reaches all the places where descendants were exported to in the "New World." The diaspora includes most of South and Central America (for example, Brazil, Venezuela, Suriname, and Mexico), the Caribbean Islands (Cuba, Haiti, Puerto Rico, Trinidad, and Tobago), and the United States (New Orleans, New York, and San Francisco). Variations of African stories can be found in many of these places, and these stories have become an integral part of the cultures of more than one hundred countries besides. The sacred orature of the diaspora is taught at universities such as Harvard and Stanford, the University of Caracas in Venezuela, and the University of the West Indies. Art exhibits are displayed at museums such as The Fowler at University of California, Los Angeles and the

---

4   The Orishas are pre-human archetypes of nature that are expressed in human personalities. They have extra-human powers and the ability to interact with people and things to affect change. Their primary function is to act as intermediaries between humans and the great one, Olodumare.

Metropolitan Museum in New York City. Related books and supplies are bestselling items on Amazon.com and other commercial outlets.

But long before this global profusion, in every traditional culture within the diaspora, our ancestors sat around a fire beneath the full moon and told stories that explained the sacredness of life, nature, and spirit. These stories provided the guidelines for inner peace, spiritual education, and communal action. The art of storytelling is the progenitor of the school, the church, and the theater. As a storyteller, I am blessed with the greatest of ancestral gifts: the ability, through the wealth of myths and folktale found in a calabash of cowries, to recount the wisdom of the ancestors and demonstrate its relevance to our present life.

Myths are stories that encode our understandings of the world, our collective histories, and our ways of being. Myth has the power to unite people across cultures by revealing the universal truths of life as they are expressed through specific sets of archetypes. In African diasporic cultures, ancient myths are called Odus, and the wisdom in the ancient stories are interpreted in the light of contemporary concerns. This means that the Odus have both an esoteric and an exoteric application. Some of these myths are the subjects of life-long study by the priests of the diaspora, while others have been simplified and are available to the laity. This accessibility to everyday people is important because everyday life in the diaspora is sacred. The myths and stories of the diaspora are embedded in children's nursery rhymes, in the recipes of holiday dinners, in bones, stones, and seeds. And everything is contained within the calabash—including, as we will see, our stories.

The calabash is the great grandmother of all containers. Today we are accustomed to shopping carts, tote bags, gift baskets, dye pots, backpacks, suitcases, soup bowls, cooking spoons, wine flasks, water bottles, musical instrument cases, and special delivery parcels. All these conveniences are the grandchildren of African material culture's calabashes, which are created from the dried and hollowed out rinds of gourds.

In the mythology of West Africa, the world itself is viewed as a covered calabash:

> "The Universe is a sphere which may be compared to two halves of a calabash, the edges of which match exactly; the join line is the line of the horizon. . . . The process of ordering the world before the creation of [humans] consisted essentially in gathering together the earth, determining the place of the waters, securing the welding together of the whole."[5]

Imagine a round gourd that has been cut in half. The horizontal line that separates the top from the bottom is the horizon. This is where we live. The top half of the calabash, Ile Orun, the heavens, contains the stars and the planets, and, most importantly, it is the dimension of the deities. Beneath the line of the earth is the realm of Olokun, the domain of the waters. In our creation story, we are told that

---

5   P. Mercier, "The Fon of Dahomey," in *African Worlds: Studies in the Cosmological Ideas and Social Values of African Peoples*, ed. Daryll Forde (Oxford, U.K.: Oxford University Press, 1954), p. 220. Quoted in *Jambalaya: The Natural Woman's Book of Personal Charms and Practical Rituals*, p. 52.

Obatala descended from the heavens on a golden chain (a beam of light) carrying a bag of soil and a five-toed hen. With these tools, the earth as we know it was created. All of creation is contained in the calabash, and although it has been cut in half to accommodate our presence, the serpent Damballah insures stability by wrapping Himself around the calabash and holding it all together. Obatala later drinks from a gourd while creating humans; Yemaya, Oya, and Oshun bring their wares to market in a calabash, and the goddess Obba presents Her life-altering soup in a calabash.

This importance of the calabash is expressed in many ceremonial ways. Healing herbs are processed in a calabash, sacred carvings adorn their exteriors, and divining tools such as cowrie shells are housed inside highly decorated gourds. These containers are presented as wedding gifts filled with intimate objects; prized possessions are placed in a calabash and buried with the body during funerals. And initiates dance with a calabash on their heads in a procession that announces the completion of their passage into the priesthood.

The importance of this symbol survived the Middle Passage and lived on in the minds and hearts of African American enslaved people. We escaped from slavery by looking to the heavens and "following the drinking gourd," which led us north to freedom.

The importance of cowrie shells has also been maintained. Cowrie shells come in several sizes and colors. Typically, there is a smooth hump on one side of the shell and a jagged side that can be regarded as the "mouth" of the shell. Cowrie shells are used as decorations for clothing, jewelry, and ceremonial objects such as the gourds mentioned above. The shells were used as currency in West Africa before colonization, as well as in several of the world's island cultures. But most importantly, the cowrie shell is the mouth of the sacred oracle.

Cowrie shells serve as the major divinatory tool of the diaspora. When the shells are cast, they fall on the divining tray in a number and pattern that contains a proverb, a myth, a prediction of future events, and a prescription for ritual actions to impact the outcome of the message from the shells. When the mouths of the shells are opened, they speak, and the voice of the ancestors is heard; the mysteries of the divine are revealed. The community is empowered to contemplate the meaning of the Odu and to apply its wisdom into their daily lives. The Odu is dynamic, accumulative, and ever-renewing.

Although the myths may be discussed at length by those who have knowledge of the inner working of the oracle, the stories born of these myths are made available to the community of the uninitiated through folklore. For example, the proverb "Nobody knows what's at the bottom of the ocean" speaks to the nature of the deity known as Olokun and reflects the mystery of the unexplored depths of the ocean and the collective unconscious. This is made accessible in our story "Olokun's Challenge."

Myths inform our cultures on every level. But the word "myth" is often misunderstood. In popular usage, the word myth refers to a falsehood. In this first definition, a myth is a body of information that is incomplete and erroneous. Perhaps there is a grain of truth in the story, but a shortage of essential "facts" leads to an erroneous conclusion. For example: "Money can buy anything." Not true! Money can buy goods and services but cannot buy good character and true love.

The second definition of myth is ethnocentric. The word is often used to describe a story that belongs to an "other." In this case, myth is regarded as a "cute little story" or the strange musing of primitive people, someone or something that is "not like us" and therefore irrelevant. This definition is poisoned by an assumption of superior intellect and knowledge and a devaluation of the inheritance of the "other" culture and its people.

The stories of the Greeks and Romans, "the old Westerns," now dominate the consciousness of popular American culture. We know Zeus, Poseidon, and Hades. We know the titans from the 1981 film *Clash of the Titans* and from the great ship the *Titanic*. The month of January is named for the god Janus, and runners in the Olympics often wear the name of the Greek goddess Nike on their feet. "Western" characters inform our political and scientific views as well. NASA launched rockets named for the Western astrological symbol of the sitting president. So, during the reign of John F. Kennedy, the rockets were named Gemini. The Apollo rockets were named for Lyndon Baines Johnson, born under the sign of Leo, which is associated with the god Apollo.

Because of the movies, we may have some superficial acquaintance with the symbols and names of the gods of Egypt—a cinematic travesty, in my opinion. We are taught to explore the desert, steal from the pyramids, and then run in fear from the mummy now awakened from the dead. Asian mythological creatures are finding favor with America's youth because of anime and manga, and other graphic literature begins to bring us some images from other countries and cultures.

But seldom do we find the myths and symbols from the stories of the African diaspora illuminated in the writing and movies of Western culture. Instead, for decades, insulting stereotypes of the mammy, the no-count watermelon-eating boy, and the promiscuous bubbling brown sugar/ "tragic mulatta" dominated the stage in minstrel shows, the television with programs like *Amos 'n Andy*, and the movies with Blaxploitation films like *Superfly*.

Among professional storytellers, there has been a predisposition among white tellers to appropriate African stories without giving credit or monetary compensation. And even some Black tellers habitually apologized for the quality (or supposed lack thereof) of our myth and folklore. They often limited their stories to life on the plantation, stories from the Bible, or Greco-Roman tales in blackface.

We are blessed to live at a time when storytellers (the most benevolent of performers) are more aware of both the universal themes common to all human life and the unique expressions of various racial and ethnic groups. I wish to praise the movie *Black Panther*, which was bold enough to present a story that incorporated important aspects of Africana culture (ancestor reverence, soul transformation, and community responsibility) without succumbing to any one-dimensional stereotypes of the cultural hero. Credit is also due to Neil Gaiman, whose vibrant work of magical realism *American Gods* invoked culturally and historically accurate portrayals of deities of the diaspora. I am inspired by these works.

But overwhelmingly our culture suffers from empty or exploitive myths. Some of them are chosen to reinforce stereotypes, to keep a class of people (women, people of color, children) in their "proper place" as "other" and inferior to those in the dominant culture. We are fooled into believing that one race of people is somehow a superhuman, superman. Their messages separate us from each other deliberately. Other stories are simply bad medicine, poorly written, directed, and produced. These narratives hypnotize people into buying unaffordable, useless objects with a false promise of soul satisfaction. These stories attack self-esteem and help to bring on alienation, addiction, depression, and even suicide.

Finally, and fatally, those stories tell us that humans are the "masters," here to exploit the natural resources of the earth. We are bombarded with the images and symbols of such stories all day, every day, everywhere. These stories lead us astray.

In order to rehumanize, we need to slow down, put down the cell phone, and turn off the television. We need to sit around an open fire with a cup of something to drink. We need to sit together across generations and cultures to share the stories that have endured for centuries and whose messages continue to have meanings for life on Earth.

The stories in this anthology originated within the calabash. They were born on the African continent, out of the collective consciousness of those ancestors. As we've seen, African mythology has a well-defined relationship to spiritual practice, and the storyteller's art is highly adaptable. There are literally tens of thousands of stories that originated on the mother continent with her diverse spiritualities, stories that remained in the minds and hearts of the people who endured the brutal journey of the Middle Passage. When these ancestors landed on the shores of the Caribbean Islands and what later became the "Americas," they brought their myths and folklore with them.

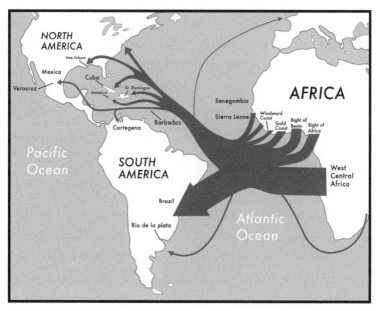

Pathways of the transatlantic slave trade
and African disaporic migration.

The stories that I've selected here come primarily from West Africa. They are found especially in Nigeria, Benin, and Ghana. Their stories of tricksters (Elegba), hunters (Ogun/Ochoosi), shape-shifters (Orunsen), and great rulers (Shango) blended with the stories of the Native people of the lands where European slavers brought them. This syncretism gave birth to the Afro-Indigenous storytelling tradition. The blending of African peoples with Native peoples and pagan Europeans under the Catholic Church is what produced African diasporic culture as it exists today in the Caribbean and the Americas.

As a priestess of African diaspora traditions, I have inherited these tales by right of blood and initiation. Most of the myths told here are housed in the sacred orature (Ese Ifa, Pataki, or Ifa poetry, proverbs, and myths), but their meaning is made available to everyday people through popular folklore. I have inherited the responsibility to contribute to the ancestral treasury of the diaspora. So, I am committed to keeping these stories alive and relevant to everyday life.

To make them accessible, enjoyable, I have treated them in two ways:

- *Composite tales*: The composite tale brings together several stories involving the same characters. I weave together a collage of tales from several cultures (e.g., Nigeria, Cuba, Haiti). This is done to present a holistic view of the characters' powers, personalities, and interactions with each other.

- *Returned tales*: The returned tales are written in contemporary language and emphasize the importance of the story to contemporary issues. I have taken the old message and turned it into the morning news. Of especial importance to me is the need to illuminate the role of the divine feminine in these stories. I have spent decades searching for the deeper meaning of the goddesses, to go beyond "the wife of so and so," the limited definition of the feminine. This is important to the women of the diaspora especially and to all women in general.

The tales included here were selected for their universal principles, their cultural richness, and their diverse messages. These are stories of loyalty, love, disappointment, betrayal, respect, wonder, and bewilderment. People of African descent and those born into the cultures of the diaspora will find information that helps us to better understand ourselves and our elders. People of other cultures in every direction will discover the stories with themes that apply to all people and will be prompted to answer the question, "What does Africa have to do with me?"

These tales will be rendered in a language and style that is accessible to all. Both those who are new to the material and those familiar with it will experience a star-studded creation story. They will dance with Damballah, the world serpent, and they will meet Elegba, the Trickster in the crossroads, among dazzling others. The proper names and pronouns of the Orishas are capitalized out of respect for Their power and Their importance. The meaning of these stories is accessible to all people of all races and backgrounds. The only requirement is that you allow your "imaginative child self" to enjoy the stories.

These stories are intended to address the entire village. Stories such as "The Wishing Star" are very friendly for young child reading these tales at nighttime. "The Two Friends" will have meaning for adolescents, and "The Division of the Cowries" may carry a lesson for rivaling teenage sisters. "The Creation" and other early life stories help us to think about the origin and meaning of life in new and varied ways, and the depictions of the relationships between the male and female characters help us to consider the challenges we find in our own relationships and rethink societal approaches to gender.

I admit that of the many tales I have performed over the decades, these are a few of my favorites. Each tale has a prologue that helps you understand the background of the story, recounting meditations in Nature that guided my interpretation of the myth and delving into some of my experiences performing the story.

As you read this book, sit around the fire in the forest or in the audience at the local school or theater. I'll join you on the couch in your living room. Hear the story's environment, smell the wind, taste the water. Adorn yourself like one of the characters and, most importantly, feel the presence of the other people listening to the story. Allow yourself to partake of the African diaspora storytelling tradition: perform call and response. In a movie house, you are restrained from calling out to the characters in the film. Here the opposite is advised. You are free to laugh out loud at Elegba, to warn Obatala to be careful, to bargain with the women in the marketplace, and to wipe away Obba's bloody tears.

Dip your hand into the calabash and pick up some cowries. The reflections, charms, and rituals found in the wisdom ways appendix are beautiful shells. I invite you to use them to integrate the universal meaning of these stories into the particular concerns of your life today.

Abundant blessing.

Yeye Teish, wordsmyth

Nedra Willliams, *Dancing Women*. 2022.

A CAST OF CHARACTERS

Agayu Sola/Aganju: The lord of the volcano. Reputed to be the father of Shango and a lover to Oshun, He is the magma in the belly of the volcano and the dry heat of the desert. When associated with flowing water, He is the ferryman who escorts us across the River of Death.

Agemo: The Chameleon. A trickster who changes His color and His temperament, He is a messenger to Obatala.

The Ajogun: The eight major (and two hundred minor) negative forces intent on disrupting the progress of humans. They are: Disease (Arun), Loss (Ofo), Paralysis (Egba), Problems (Oran), Curse (Epe), Imprisonment (Ewon), and Confusion (Wahala).

Damballah/Ayida Hwedo: The rainbow serpent whose body holds the calabash of the world in place. Wrapping from the bottom of the ocean to the height of the sky, Damballah makes a full circle by placing His tail in His mouth. Sometimes this task is fulfilled by a tail-in-mouth joining of Damballah and Ayida Hwedo. Both are well worshiped in Haiti.

Elegba/Legba/Eshu: The Trickster and the master of the crossroads. He represents chaos, chance, and contradiction. He is the trickster-magician-linguist. He is often depicted as a spoiled child or a crippled old man. Most often He is seen wearing a chest plate of cowrie shells. In the most elegant sculptures of Elegba, He wears a penis-shaped cap covered in cowrie shells. His colors are black, white, and red. His number is three.

Elusu: A mermaid mostly known in Brazil. She is described as "chalk white" because She lives deep in the ocean where the sun does not shine.

Iku: Death. He roams the earth looking for food, which includes plants, animals, humans, and even Orishas. He is tall and muscular and has white dots all over His deep black body. He moves stealthily, has a strong odor of decay, and is surrounded by buzzing flies. Oya is his best friend.

Iya Nla: Iya Nla, mother vast as the sky, is the mother of all creation who is responsible for the material manifestation of spirit in the natural world and for the existence of human beings. She gives us our identity as humans, our ancestral lineage, the power of prophecy through Odu, and our ability to relate to spirit in our human form. She is envisioned as both ancient and ever-renewing. Artists have portrayed Her as a stately woman with luminous white hair braided and wrapped around the top of Her head like a crown. She can be concealed in the inner recesses of women's bodies or revealed in the movements of the clouds.

Inle/Erinle: A hunter on land and in the sea. Associated with the estuary, an in-between space where the freshwater river meets the salty sea, He is a deity of health and serves as a physician for other deities.

Iya Mapo: A great mother associated with the moisture of the earth. She is the water that wet the clay as Obatala/Iya Nla shaped the bodies of humans. She is a miner who digs for clay, a sculptor who shapes pots, and a scientist who controls fire as She glazes and fires the pots. She is the matron-mother of women's craft societies, weavers, dye and soap makers, oil producers, and potters. Her color is purple.

Nana Buluku/Nana Buruku: The primordial mother of the Fon people of Dahomey and the Yoruba of Nigeria. She is the cosmic force that produced the divine twins, Mawu-Liza, the moon and the sun. After giving birth, She retired to the upper realms of the universe. Her power is contained in the calabash of creation. She is envisioned as a dignified elder woman and is addressed as Grandmother. She is associated with swamplands and watches over the doorway between life and death. Her gift is serenity. She is celebrated in many cultures. In the Caribbean (Haiti and Suriname), in South America (Brazil), and even in Europe (France and Holland). Stories about Her can be found in places touched by the transatlantic slave trade. Her color is pink.

Obatala: The King of the White Cloth and the deity who sets our ethical standards. He shapes the child in the womb and rules the head. His primary color is luminous white with silver, purple, or orange beadwork. He carries a white switch made of horsehair and cowrie shells. He is envisioned as a stately and slow old man but can become vigorous in battle. His virtues are humility, patience, modesty, and humor. His faults are conceit and arrogance. His number is eight.

Obba: Shango's appointed wife, affiliated with the Obba River. A strong but quiet woman, She is orderly, frugal, diligent, and accommodating. She wears a simple garment with a large head wrap of pink, red, or lilac fabric. She rules the home and endures the challenges of daily life. Her virtues are discipline and devotion. Her weaknesses are misplaced compassion and self-sabotage.

Ochoosi: A deity of the forest. A tracker who hunts with a bow and arrow, He is slender and handsome, courteous and quiet. He teaches us to tread lightly on the path to spiritual development.

Ogun: The wildman in the woods. He represents material civilization, labor, and warfare. He is the toolmaker, the blacksmith, and the hunter. He is envisioned as a black-skinned man who is exceptionally muscular. A hard worker, there is a slight sadness in His eyes. He is bare chested and wears a grass overskirt. He carries a machete and, as the blacksmith, He works at an anvil and with fire. He is reclusive and moody. Exceptional ability in warfare is His virtue; uncontrolled violence is His vice. His colors are black and green. His number is three.

Olokun: The owner of the deep, the bottom of the ocean. A merman with a split tail, He is keeper of all the wealth at the bottom of the sea and the primordial waters. All the water on the earth flows from Olokun.

Although Olokun is regarded as male in Benin, where he is well worshipped, the female aspect of the deep ocean is identified as **Yemidirigbe** in neighboring Yorubaland. She is a mermaid with pale skin, sparkling eyes, and green seaweed hair. She is sometimes envisioned wearing a "beard of authority."

In the diaspora, They are merged into an androgynous/gynandrous[6] deity and referred to as Yemaya-Olokun.

Oludumare: Olodumare is the transcendent force that created the entire universe. Colonial misinterpretation refers to Olodumare as "he," but in Yoruba cosmology, this force exists beyond embodiment, has no sex, no images, no shrines, and no priests. Olodumare relates to the world through the intercessions of the celestial Orishas Olorun, "the owner of heaven," or Olofin, "the owner of the sun." Although Olodumare is distant from Earth and aloof from the affairs of humans, you'll see in our tales that Olodumare scrutinizes the behavior of the Orishas who have been assigned to guide and direct life on planet Earth.

Orisha Oko: The deity of agriculture. He is envisioned as a farmer who drives an ox-drawn plow. Orisha Oko represents those times in human history when people move from being hunter-gathers to being settled caretakers of the land.

Orunmila: The deity of divination, owner of the Ifa oracle, and the witness to creation. He is envisioned as a very dig-

---

6   When the primarily female deity (gyn) has within it a male (andros) aspect. When androgynous, the primarily male deity (andros) has a female aspect within it.

nified prophet who travels around the world disseminating the wisdom and the wishes of Olodumare. He is the ordained husband of Oshun.

Osain: The deity of the wild herbs of the forest. He is a dwarf with one eye, one arm, and one leg who can see more, do more, and dance better than those with two. He is dedicated to healing but is also a reclusive trickster.

Oshun: The goddess of love, beauty, wealth. The owner of the Oshun River and the town of Oshogbo, She is the creatrix of culture and is Shango's lover. She is envisioned as an exceptionally beautiful woman: shapely and voluptuous with alluring eyes, full red lips, and uplifted breasts. She dresses in the finest cloth with bright patterns in yellow, green, and orange. She wears gold and brass bangles on Her wrists and arms, tiny bells around Her ankles, and a skirt of five yellow silk scarves. She speaks in a honey tone, using seductive language. She is a superior cook, singer, and dancer. Creativity, generosity, and kindness are Her virtues. When offended, She can be unforgiving and vengeful. Her number is five.

Oya: The wildwoman, the force of lightning, the ruler of the marketplace, the queen of the winds of change, the boss-lady of the cemetery. Associated with the Niger River, She is Shango's running partner. She is tall and slender, light on Her feet. Her features are sharp, and light flows from Her eyes. Her hair of long black locs is adorned with striped beads and copper lightning bolts. Her necklace is made of nine masks. She wears a grass skirt or one made of nine colors, with a pair of loose-fitting pants underneath.

She carries a sword and a long, brown locust bean rattle. Her virtues are independence and self-authority. Her faults are a hair-trigger temper and erratic change. Her number is nine.

Shango: The ruler of the powerful kingdom of Oyo. The son of Obatala, He is both the lord of thunder and the spirit of humans, ego, and political organization. He is envisioned as a dark-brown-skinned man with alluring eyes and a winning smile. He is attractive, sexy, and charming. His virtue is courage. His colors are red and white. He is hot tempered with a thundering voice. He carries a double-headed axe. He is always victorious in battle. When He speaks, fire flows from His mouth. He wears a crown of turtle shell beads and carries a bag of magical items on His cowrie shell belt. He owns a striking white horse. His number is six.

Timi and Gbonka: The heads of Shango's army and police force. They are blood brothers. They represent law enforcement and loyalty. They are healthy young men trained in combat and community service.

Yemaya/Yemonja/Yemona/Yemiderigbe: The mother of all the Orishas. The goddess of the ocean, domestic authority, fertility, and nurturance, She is envisioned as a lovely woman, large breasted and black skinned with penetrating eyes. She wears a skirt made of seven layers of fabric in different shades of blue. Her crown is adorned with seashells and silver beads. Her virtues are tolerance and nurturance. Her flaws are hypersensitivity and resentment. Her number is seven. She is sometimes known as Yemiderigbe.

Yewa: An angel of the night. Once a beautiful woman, She chose celibacy to avoid the gaze of Shango the womanizer. She is chaste, pious, lonely, and childless. She is a mortician who lives in the cemetery and oils the bodies of the dead. She is a friend to Iku (Death), Oya, and Obba.

Nedra Williams, *As Above, So Below (2)*. 2022.

PART I:
THE CALABASH

THE CREATION

Every culture has a creation story. They vary greatly. Creation stories were designed to explain the coming of material reality and to guide the behavior of human beings in relationship to it. In this rendition, I have integrated elements from several myths found in the diaspora. Note that according to African belief, the snake is not an evil creature. Instead, He represents the depository of ancestral memory.

In the beginning, at a time when there was no time, all that existed was the great silence in the dark depth of the cosmic womb, Nana Buluku. Within the womb, Olodumare, the great egg of the world, sat in patient potential waiting for the fated moment of its hatching. Suddenly a sound burst out from the center of the egg: *OOORR-RROOO.* Then, the life-giving particles in the egg quickened and set into motion a tremendous bang, causing creative air spirits to dance among themselves in the form of gases.

Some danced themselves into fire.

Others clashed and collided into the fireballs spinning through the deep blue of space. In the frenzy of their joy, Mawu the Moon and Liza the Sun were born.

They leaped and tumbled together and formed Yemaya-Olokun, the ocean. Then great masses of land erupted from Her depth,[7] forming the earth. The rushing hum of the ocean splashed itself against Earth's shores.

Sun stepped forward to perform His solo, and the Moon laid back to cool Herself off in the Upper Deep. As the Sun performed His slow drag over the surface of the earth, life stirred in His rays. In the depth of the sea, things began to form: a single cell divided into two, making seaweed, hydra, and fish. The crab crawled out of the water and found that on the land, life was moving. Seeds burst open, forming flowers, trees, and fruit. Spiders crawled, birds flew, and bush cows roamed in the forest.

A blazing heat permeated the earth, causing all things to stir and take shape. But the Sun's heat was overwhelming; things were being overdone. So He receded, and the Moon brought forth Her dance. She circled slowly through the night sky, cooling the earth, settling the seed, calming the waters, and leaking a mysterious ray of subtle light, Ache, that tempered everything on Earth.

The Moon called out, alarmed by the magnitude of the work They had done. Her cry resounded to the depths of the earth, and up from the center came the rainbow serpent, Damballah Hwedo. The serpent wrapped Himself

---

7   The African belief is that there is an "Ocean in the Sky," that both Ocean and Sky are made of the same substance, but in different proportions.

around the earth and the sky, holding the two together like a covered calabash.

Sun and Moon smiled at the work of the serpent. Within His ring of power, the celestial couple made love and brought into being all the deities in pairs, twins in all things. On the planet's surface below, the palm and banana trees swayed in the wind, birds sang, fish swam, and the bush cows roamed in the garden.

THE COMING OF THE ORISHAS

The beginning of the world and the birth of the deities are often told in a series of stories that seem to contradict each other. The Greeks speak of a chaotic force that contains several beings who then fight and kill each other until a trinity (Zeus, Poseidon, Hades) is formed. Then they fight with each other until one of them, Zeus, is declared supreme. The Egyptian pantheon is created when two divine beings (Geb and Nuit) mate and produce many other gods.

In Dahomey/Benin we find a self-generating mother goddess (Nana Buluku) who gives birth to a pair of twins (Mawu-Liza), a divine couple who then gives birth to a host of deities. The Yoruba story of the birth of the Orishas has a different cast of characters. Eventually I'll elaborate on that story in "The Day Her Belly Burst."

Here, now, is my retelling of the coming of the Orishas.

In those ancient beginnings, when the earth was new and the sky still bright with fire, there came a way of being. The energy that rested in the cell of All Potential began to shape itself and move about in space. The rainbow children who emanated from the mating of Nana and Olodumare danced across the sky.

Olorun, the owner of the blue sky, searched for His sister-mate Odudua, but He could not see the great black earth. So He called Obatala, the King of the White Cloth, the clouds. Obatala moved His robes and produced a beam of clear light. From the lightning, Oya, the goddess of the winds of change, appeared. She danced in the hem of Obatala's white robes, lining the clouds in hues of purple and pink. A roar of thunder followed the lightning, and the sky burned a blazing red as Shango announced His becoming. A tropical storm raged in the sky as Oya and Shango made love behind the clouds.

Obatala cast His light upon the darkness below and saw the surface of a watery depth. The rainbow serpent Damballah plunged Himself deep into these waters and returned with an unutterable message rolling from His tongue. He could only curl, dance, and wrap Himself around Himself, then plunge into the depth a dozen times until it was understood what must be done.

Obatala stretched His cloud body beyond the blue of the day sky and brushed Himself against Mawu the Moon, thereby collecting stardust for the assignment He now intended to carry out. Liza the sun, wanting to participate further in this act of continuous creation, sent a glittering stream of golden light for Obatala's descent to Earth.

As Obatala surfed down the sunray, Oya gave Him a five-toed hen dark as the night, yet spotted with the light of day. Obatala dropped the bag of stardust upon the waves of the deep sea and let loose the guinea hen. She scratched and scratched until she created another dimension, a place for the gods to live. Now Odudua could be seen in Her dark glory!

Damballah looked upon this work of theirs and plunged Himself into the depths again. This time He carried a message which was understood by those who lay waiting in the deep, dark waters. From that watery womb came Olokun, the mudfish-god, and Yemaya, the mother of the children of the sea, riding a great wave into the light of day. The crashing waves disturbed the sleep of Aganju the volcano. As He stretched and yawned, hot lava rushed down the mountain, and its ash filled the air. Oya joined in this dance and hurled lightening for miles in every direction, creating forest fires that attracted the attention of the wild one, Ogun.

Osain, the god of herbs, played tag with Ogun. They ran like little boys up and down the valleys, over the mountains, and across the plains, turning all green in their wake. There was so much activity, so much dancing. The wind sang in the trees, the water splashed a varied rhythm, and the thunder accented the changing tempo of the dance.

For a moment the deities stilled themselves, the scent of wildflowers and honey drifting softly on a gentle breeze. Then They felt something silky and smooth upon their skins. Now each deity moved in a new way, undulating as They wondered what was coming over Them.

The forest bowed as the sun's light brightened. Salt surrendered to sand, and sweet water cascaded down the mountainside. A chorus of birds sang in the sky; in the river, water lilies blossomed. The deities looked at each other with increased desire. What was this amazing thing emerging from the mystery of creation?

As the river rolled across the land, and gold dust sprinkled the air, there in that mist appeared a wondrous sight:

Black buttocks adorned
in white cowrie shells,
used to divine and as money.
Curly hair thick, long liana vines,
bouncing breasts glistening
with honey.
Eyes sparkling bright
like the stars in the night.
A sweet voice that beckons and thrills.
Beauty and grace,
an enchanting embrace,
and a love
that can cure and can kill.

"I am Oshun," said the beautiful being. "The blessing of Olodumare is in Me."

The deities understood and rejoiced now that love had come to be.

Nedra Williams, *Oshun*. 2022.

OSHUN LEARNS THE ART OF DIVINING

The story of how cowrie shells came to be used for divination varies from one level of orature to another. The divining system known as Ifa uses sixteen kola nuts (ikin) or a divining chain (opele) with eight coins to receive the proverb, myth, prediction, and prescription that address the seeker's concern. The prophet Orunmila owns the Ifa system of divination.

Ifa speaks of a time when Oshun was the wife of Orunmila. In that myth, Orunmila travels from town to town, divining for the royalty of each village. So, He is seldom home. While He is on the road, His wife Oshun is left to face the many needs and demands of the local people who come to seek divination. It's said that She created the oracle known as dilloggun to meet those demands.

In the mythology of the popular culture, it is Obatala (the King of the White Cloth) who holds all the knowledge. In this story Elegba the Trickster creates a situation whereby Oshun can acquire the coveted knowledge held by Obatala. The nature of these three Orishas (Obatala, Elegba, and Oshun), their relationship to each other, and their role in the dissemination of knowledge is revealed in this charming story.

Maferefun Oshun.

In the beginning, only Obatala, the King of the White Cloth, the ruler of intellect and ethics—only He knew the art of divining. Only He could cast the palm nuts, the kola, and the cowrie shells to read the will of destiny. Only He knew the predictions and the prescriptions to guide the flow of life.

Every day, Oshun, the goddess of the river, asked Him, "Baba will you teach me the art of divining?"

And every day Obatala said, "No, Oshun, you're too young. No, Oshun, you're too pretty. No, Oshun, you're too silly."

Well, one day the King of the White Cloth took off His white cloth and got into the river to bathe. While He was languishing in the water, along came Elegba the Trickster, who snatched up Obatala's clothes and beat a path to His hut.

That morning, Oshun was out picking wildflowers when She came upon Obatala bathing in the river. "Good morning, Baba," she said.

"Good morning, daughter."

"Are things well with you this morning, Baba?"

Obatala replied things were just fine—yet as He reached for His white cloth to cover Himself, He discovered that His great clouds were gone. Obatala covered Himself with His hands and informed Oshun that someone had taken His clothes.

Oshun replied, "So?"

"Without my clothing, I cannot come out of the river."

"Why not?"

"Because I'm naked," He cried. "Oshun, you don't understand. What is the King of the White Cloth without His white cloth?"

It was then that She understood the magnitude of His dilemma. Oshun looked around for the cloth of the king, and there She spotted the footprints of the Trickster!

Suddenly She was visited by a bright idea. "Baba, if I recover Your clothes for You, will You teach Me the art of divining?"

Obatala replied that He would do anything to cover His awesome power.

"Stay here; I'll be right back," Oshun answered as She chuckled to Herself.

She ran to Her hut, and She used Her magic formula (*don't miss this formula, sisters*): She bathed Herself in river water, smeared Her tongue, breast, and clitoris with honey, and wrapped Her hips in five yellow silk scarves. Then She followed the footprints of the Trickster to His hut.

When She arrived at Elegba's hut, She stood in the doorway so that the sunlight glistened on the honey on the tips of Her breast just so.

Elegba was just about to hide Obatala's cloth in the rafters when Oshun called His name in a honeyed voice.

Elegba turned around, and suddenly He was overcome with a hunger for honey. When Elegba saw Her standing there in the sunlight, His tongue fell down His chin as the power between His thighs began to rise.

He called for honey, plainly at first.

She asked for clothes, as a matter of fact.

A drop of honey fell on His finger. He placed it in His mouth.

The skirt of yellow scarves fell from Her waists.

He fell on His knees before Her, hungering for the taste of honey.

The bells on Her ankles tinkled. She reached for Obatala's clothes.

Finally, They compromised.

Oshun returned to the river and gave Obatala His spotless white cloth.

And, being a deity of His word, Obatala began to teach Oshun the art of divining.

For sixteen days and sixteen nights, He taught Her how to cast, and for sixteen days and sixteen nights, He taught Her how to read.

And when She had learned all the invocations, all the proverbs, the myths, and incantations; when She could read all the predictions; when She could mark all the prescriptions; when She could mix all the powders and potions; when She could sing all the songs and say all the prayers; when She was sure that Her knowledge, wisdom, and understanding were complete, She called all the other Orishas together and taught Them all how to divine, absolutely free.

And since that day, Oshun, the goddess of the river, has been appealed to for love, sexuality, fertility, and abundance.

Oshun is a beautiful Orisha indeed.

OSE OTURA

Within the sacred orature of the Yoruba diaspora, we have an amazing story called "Ose Otura." It speaks to the importance of the divine feminine in the shaping of the world and the requirement that She be respected to generate creativity and to maintain balance in the world.

Because of the power of "Ose Otura," it is often said that when opposed, Oshun need not "wrinkle Her face" to defeat an enemy. She simply needs to withdraw, and the negative energy is nullified. However, this story shows that the world suffers severely in Her absence.

When Oshun withdraws, we see environmental devastation, the decay of human culture, and spiritual desolation. All can be restored by calling upon Her, respecting Her, and changing our behavior. Yet it is often said that She is the goddess of second chances, but not of thirds.

Maferefun Oshun.

As instructed by Olodumare, a party of deities descended from Ile Orun, the heavenly realm, onto Ile Aiye, the planet Earth.

This party consisted of Obatala, the King of the White Cloth, the lord of the clouds; Ogun, the wildman in the woods; and Shango, the lord of the flame.

Oshun, the goddess of sweet water, was the only female among Them.

Obatala, Shango, and Ogun spoke among Themselves, declaring the great works They would achieve.

Obatala declared, "I will release rain from my luminous clouds to fall gently upon the earth." In his zeal, the King missed the look of irritation that came across the lovely Oshun's face.

Then Ogun speculated, "I'll explore the forest and find the materials to create tools."

And Shango announced, "I shall simply rule over it all to ensure that We, the deities, are properly praised."

Oshun said nothing. Instead, She walked around the three men and looked Them up and down, contemplating Her contribution to the creative process.

Obatala grew impatient with Her contemplation. Ogun was eager to get to work, and Shango demanded, "Make up your mind right now!"

But Oshun refused to be rushed or bullied by Them. "My guidance don't come from You, and neither does my rain. I'll do what I do when I do it."

Obatala recommended that They proceed.

"We don't need You," Shango told Oshun.

The goddess waved Her little finger at Them. "You shall see" is all She said. Then She took a seat in the curve of the crescent moon, looked in the mirror, and began to powder Her face.

As She did so, all the sweet water on the earth dried up.

Obatala discovered that He could not spin dry clay—He needed water to make human beings. And without sweet water to fertilize the forest, Ogun found no fiber and had nothing with which to make tools. Shango was truly dismayed because, with no material goods and no one to rule over, He felt completely useless. When They realized that They couldn't create anything, They ran back to Olodumare, the owner of the day, and complained: "Why did you send us down there? We can't accomplish nothing."

Olodumare stroked His chin. "First of all, somebody's missing from this crew that I sent down there. Where is Oshun?"

And one of the fools said, "Well, you know, who needs Her?"

With displeasure, Olodumare commanded, "Shut up, sit still, and learn something."

Oshun had just been chilling on the moon, waiting for Them to realize that nothing was happening. But when the Great One summoned Oshun, She arrived and took Her seat at the feet of Olodumare.

He asked Her, "Why are you not among Them?"

When She replied, Her words flowed like honey, sensuous and unhurried. "They insulted Me. With Their sense of power and privilege, and without contemplation, They rushed to dominate the earth. They assumed They didn't need fresh water; They didn't need sensuality; They didn't need love."

Olodumare glared at the three of Them. "Are you stupid?"

They were silent.

"Do you assume I don't know what *I'm* doing?"

They were silent.

"Do you not know that She makes life worth living?"

They were silent.

Shango attempted to say something, but Olodumare commanded, "Apologize. Right now!"

Obatala lowered His head and said, "I beg your pardon."

Ogun rung His hands and said, "I'm so sorry."

Shango looked directly in Her eyes and asked, "Can you forgive me?"

Each of Them promised to change to be Their better selves.

Oshun conferred with Olodumare. He asked Her to be merciful, for the sake of creation.

She considered His request and Their respective assignments. For the sake of creation, She granted, "Yes, I accept your apologies. But don't let it happen again."

And She was satisfied . . . for the moment.

Oshun had been Olodumare's primary messenger, something the gods had to learn. But this incident made Her question that role—She really didn't want to be bothered with such behavior. Deep inside Herself, She meditated on a solution to the problem.

As She did, Her belly expanded like the full moon.

Then Oshun gave birth to a male child: Elegba, and She assigned *Him* to carry all the messages between heaven and earth.

THE DAY HER BELLY BURST

Many early versions of this tale speak of a time when Yemaya held all the water of the earth in Her belly. We are told that Ogun expressed His attraction to Her by chasing Her with the intent to rape. She ran from Him. She fell, and when Her belly burst, the singular body of water turned into rivers, lakes, and streams. Sometimes this tale, along with the behavior of certain mammals, was recounted to insinuate that "rape is a natural act," supporting and normalizing a rape culture.

Rape is a serious violation of the body and a wound to the human spirit. Healing from rape requires deep and long-term work.

While meditating on Yemaya's image at my altar, I felt the presence of a benevolent mother. I made offerings at the Pacific Ocean under the moon and marveled at the shimmering light, the movement of the waves, and the rocks that formed islands in the water. This vision of loveliness and the feeling of power gave me the courage to interrogate the use and the true meaning of the myth. On my seventh ocean visit, I promised Her that I would create an alternative story to heal the negative social effects of this tale.

The purest meaning of myths are expressions of the observed behavior of nature. I pondered that if Yemaya represented a unified body of water, and Ogun (in His natural state) represented the untamed mountain forests of the earth, perhaps this was really a story about the eruption of land penetrating the waters. As the land erupts, islands emerge. The water falls down the mountains, splashes into the caves, and creates rapids in the crevices of the river. Such tumultuous activity could be imagined as "The Day Her Belly Burst."

This reinterpretation of the tale was given to me during my meditations with Yemaya. It is designed to celebrate Her beauty and to strengthen the bond between Her and the women of the world. I have enacted this story for and with survivors of childhood sexual abuse, rape, and domestic battery. The only prop is a large round mirror. I invite the women in the audience to gaze upon their own faces and see the beauty of Yemaya.

Once upon a time there was a beautiful woman by the name of Yemaya. She looked into the waters of the ocean, and there She saw Her own reflection, and She said, "Who is that beautiful woman? I thought that *I* was the most wonderful thing that the world had ever seen!"

And as She looked upon that woman, there came a rumbling in Her belly, and it grew, and it grew, and it grew till it exploded and sprinkled the night with stars and a full moon.

Yemaya looked into the light of the moon, and there She saw Her own reflection, and She asked, "Who is that beautiful woman? I thought that *I* was the prettiest thing that the world had ever seen!"

And as She looked upon that woman, there came a rumbling in Her belly, and it grew, and it grew, and it grew till it exploded and covered the earth with rivers, lakes, and streams.

Yemaya looked into the waters of the lake, and there She saw Her own reflection, and She cried, "Who is that beautiful woman? I thought that *I* was the finest thing that the world had ever seen!"

And as She looked upon that woman, there came a rumbling in Her belly, and it grew, and it grew, and it grew till it exploded, and before Her stood thousands of beautiful women!

"Who are you beautiful women?" She exclaimed. "I thought that *I* was the loveliest thing that the world had ever seen!"

And the women looked deep into the eyes of Yemaya, and there they saw their own reflections, and they said to Her: "You are, Momma. We are just You."

MOTHER OF THE NIGHT

In the mid-nineties I was pleased to be a faculty member at the University of Creation Spirituality (directed by Dr. Matthew Fox). Often the faculty traveled to various location to conduct classes.

One summer, we visited the University of British Columbia in Vancouver. I taught a dance as meditation class in the totem pole room of the museum. It was wonderful moving across the floor beneath the towering totem poles. One particular pole depicted a female figure with a variety of land animals, sea creatures, birds, and bugs issuing from Her body. The ID placard read "Mother of the Night."

When I came home, I sat in front of my Yemaya altar. It seemed that a large opening, a vertical hole, surrounded and contained me. I was neither asleep nor awake. I could feel my hand moving but did not see what I was writing until I exited the vertical hole.

This is the poem I wrote while in that trance.

I am the Mother of the Night.

The Great Dark Depth, the Bringer of Light.

All that was, that is, that ever shall be,

all that could or should can only come from me.

High above and far below. I am the ebb, I am the flow.

The stars in the sky, the fish in the sea.

Every seed,
every stone,
every critter is me.

I am the Center, the Beginning, the End. I am without
and I am within. I am the lair, the nest, and the den.
I am the Earth, the Water, and Wind.

The Horned Cow, the many-teated Sow, the Queen bee,
the Mothertree, the Pregnant Womb, the Grain-seed
    broom,
the candle's wick, the matrix, and woman, you are
my daughter.

Praise and Love to the Mothers of the World.

Praise and Love to the Sisters of the World.

Praise and Love to the Women of the World.

Praise and Love to my daughters.

To the women in the fields, who plow and plant and turn
mill wheels. To those who spin and weave at looms,
who make the mats, the cloth and brooms. To those
who sew the royal robes, to those who pierce
the child's earlobes. To those who rub and oil
and braid. To all the Queens and all the Maids.

Praise and Love to my daughters.

To those who nurse babes on their breasts,
who carry on without due rest. Then rise up early
as the dawn to mend the fence and mow the lawn.
To those who mix and stir the pot, to those
who bake and clean and mop, to those who have
and who have not.

Praise and Love to my daughters.

Praise and Love to those who seek, to those who know,
and those who speak. To those who smile with tender eyes,
whose wisdom penetrates the lies. To those who sing
and those who cry. For those who fight for right and die!
To those who live to ripe old age, to Great Grandma, the
    family sage. Praise and Love to my daughters.

To those unborn and yet to come, we bid you on
with song and hum. From other worlds and through birth-
water, come forth, child, beloved daughter.

Praise and Love to the Mothers of the World.

Praise and Love to the Sisters of the World.

Praise and Love to the Women of the World.

Praise and Love to my daughters.

WHY THE SUN AND THE MOON LIVE IN THE SKY

This story can be found in the folklore of many people; it is told in many lands and languages, including in the folklore of Africa, China, South America, and many of the world's island cultures. It is a "cute little story," but it explains the behavior of the lights above and the waters of the earth. My particular telling of it is based on the West African version of the tale; however, I have rendered it in an African American tongue and attitude.

In the beginning, Luna, the moon, and Mare, the ocean, were the very best of friends. Every month, when the moon was full, Luna would sit just above the horizon to visit Her friend for three nights.

Then there came a night, for some unknown reason, when the two friends began to pull away from each other! Maybe Luna was just full of herself; maybe Mare had become salty and swollen. To this day, we have no idea of what really happened. We just know it caused the friends to become tense and irritable with each other.

So, one day, Luna said, "Mare, I always come to You. Why don't You ever come to Me?"

"Oh Luna, Luna, I'd love to," Mare answered, "but I'm afraid that Your house isn't big enough for Me and all My children."

Well, that felt like a splash in Her face. So Luna snapped back, "You are welcome to come to My house at any time."

"Are You sure about that, Luna?"

The moon beamed back. "I am absolutely positive." She went dark for a few days after that.

The water laid still, waiting for the renewed moon to reappear.

When Mare saw the new moon crescent, She sent up a gentle wave. The water swelled, and the cutest little fish swam around Luna's ankles.

Luna smiled to herself and called out, "Can You send more of Your children up here?"

"Of course I can." And with another wave, water came up to Luna's knees and wrapped Her legs in seaweed.

Mare laughed and called, "How d'You like that, Luna?"

Luna ripped the seaweed from around Her legs and challenged the mermaid to provide something a little more exciting.

So Mare sent a wave full of colorful fish.

Luna examined the spotted fish, the striped fish; some were black as night, and others shimmered silver.

Luna yawned. "Children of the night sky. I have so many like these."

This made Mare very angry, so She sent a pod of dolphins that danced in the water around Luna's breasts.

"Your children seem to be hungry," said Luna sarcastically. Then She dismissed the dolphins with a "Go play."

Now Mare was furious, and a tidal wave of whales pounded the water with their tails, just beneath Luna's nose.

At this point, Luna ran to Her husband, Sol, and complained about the violence happening on Earth. "Can you help me out here?"

Sol knew that this was an argument between women, and He didn't want to get involved. So, using just a few sunbeams, He extended the cover of the sky and invited Luna to chill out on the roof.

Sitting on top of the world and full now, She called down to Mare, "Keep sending Your children. There's lots of room in My house."

Mare retreated into the depths of the ocean. Luna sat on Her luminous roof.

The two women said little to each other for about a million years.

Sol, who'd decided to just stay out of it, made the sun rise in the morning and set in the evening. He left the rule of night to Luna and Mare.

Meanwhile, the children of the ocean and the children of the sky played together happily, mingling in the mirrored darkness of the night sea and sky. Despite their mothers' silence, they were having a wonderful time.

Seeing the joy of the children made the women realize that this was a contest neither of Them could win. So, eventually, Mare relented, and Luna did too. They called the children together and explained it was time to go home now.

The waters became calm, the seaweed swayed in rhythm with the waves, and the many-colored fish got good grades in school. It seemed as if everything was fine.

But as Mare looked around, She realized some of Her children were missing. Some of them were still playing around in the sky.

"You all better come on home," She called.

Luna granted, "It's all right, Mare, they'd like to play a little longer, but I'll send them home at the crack of dawn."

And for just a second, Mare was tempted to demand Her children *now*. But instead, She smiled and said okay.

The children played all night, and that morning Sol escorted them out of the sky. They landed, resentfully, on Earth.

Now I know that you've seen them, the ones who did a sleep-in at Auntie Luna's house. You've seen them. Sometimes, when you are walking along the beach, you look down, and there they are: they're the ones called starfish.

Because of these children, Luna and Mare have the best relationship now. They remember the dispute, and They laugh. Sometimes They dance together at high tide and low tide. And Sol, who doesn't want to get in between those two women now any more than He did back then, stays up in the sky and minds His own business.

Now, there is still some debate about what caused that rift between Luna and Mare in the first place. Some folks say it was the Trickster's doing. Others blamed it on Olokun.

All I know is what I was told. And now I done told it to you.

OBATALA'S MISTAKE

This is the story of "Obatala's Mistake," returned for modern times. In the original tale, Obatala, the maker of humans, drinks palm wine during the creation process. He becomes so drunk that humans are created with congenital deformities, bone malformations, and hereditary mental diseases.

In Yoruba culture, people with these conditions are sacred to Obatala and can be found congregating in front of His shrine in Ile Ife, where they receive donations of food and money.

Food scarcity leads to malnutrition; in pregnancy, polluted water contaminates the bodies of children; the cruelty of conquest and colonialism lead to transgenerational trauma. These may account for the content of the original tale.

But the deformities of our time are violence, greed, hatred, and the "Ism Brothers." So, I have created a returned tale to preserve this myth's original meaning and to emphasize its meaning and relevance for modern times. Here the creation of humans is shared between Iya Nla (the divine feminine) and Obatala (the sacred masculine).

Please, be one of the children of the "first, sober making." Help us to preserve life on Earth.

Oh well, you may not remember Me. I'm forty days older than dust. I was there at the very beginning. I'm the one who raised the mountain up and set the valley low.

You see, in the beginning, there was just the two of Us: Me, Iya Nla, and the old man, Obatala.

One day He went all over the universe, throwing stars and planets and doing whatall. And then He looked down and saw that blue ball, the one y'all now call Earth. But back then, it was covered in water, and He got a mind to come down on a glittering chain of golden light with a bag of soil and a five-toed hen. And He dropped that soil on the water, and the hen scratched the continents into place.

A few trees grew up; volcanos erupted; things like that were going on, and He made a few animals. It looked pretty good to Him, so He decided to go on about His business.

And I said, "Oh, oh, Baba? Oh, don't You think something else needs doing here?"

And He said, "Well, if You think so, Iya, do it Yourself."

So, I took a great big calabash, and I got some dirt from the north and the south and the east and the west, and I poured in ocean, river, and rain. I mixed that clay, tossed that clay, and I pinched, twisted, and patted that clay. And then I shaped it.

And when I looked at my sculpture, I had made the model of a human being! And the first ones were kind, intelligent, and beautiful.

I was so proud of Myself, I sat the down on that planet, and I sang.

Well, it was so much fun that I went over to a palm tree, and I tapped Myself a jug of palm wine, and I drank some. *Gulp, gulp, gulp.*

And then I gathered up some more clay. And I twisted and turned and patted and shaped. Then I formed some more human beings.

Well, this next batch of humans were kind but not so intelligent. But that was okay because they were beautiful. I took another drink. *Gulp, gulp, gulp.*

Then I took up more clay, and oh, I twisted and turned and tossed, and I shaped them, and I put them down, and . . . oh well, at least they were kind.

So I took another drink (*gulp, gulp, gulp*).

And I took up more clay, and I pinched and twisted and shaped and slapped, and I put it down, and . . .

Well, you get the (hiccup) picture, don't you?

And then I fell into a drunken stupor, and I slept for a million years.

While I was asleep, Baba came along. He looked at all these clay figures, and He scratched His beard and said, "Well, I guess this is what She wants." And so He took a deep breath and blew the breath of life into all My creatures.

Many, many years passed, and I slept and slept and slept until I heard a noise. It was a loud sound, like a scream.

I opened my eyes, and I looked down at this planet and— and there were all My creations, and they were yelling and screaming at each other!

All My creations were throwing sticks and rocks at each other. *My creations* began to tear down the trees—*My* creations, *My* creations were killing the animals!

I ran to Baba, and I said, "Baba! Do You see what's happening on Earth? What shall We do?"

He said, "We? They're *Your* creations. You do what You want to with them."

I looked down at the humans and I said, "You all, please, please stop fighting. Please stop fussing. Please stop killing. Please stop destroying."

But they didn't hear Me.

I said, "Please, stop. I gave you life, and I'll take it away!"

And just as I raised the finger that would destroy *all* of creation, I heard a sweet sound—somebody laughed.

And I saw one of My creatures who was strong helping one who was weak. And one who had plenty was giving to one who had nothing. And yet another was planting trees and helping animals. And then I heard a wondrous sound of musical instruments and voices singing, and people were dancing.

And I said, "Oh, oh, are *you* the children of the first, sober making?"

And someone said, "Yes, Iya."

I said, "Are you the ones who will help those in need?"

And that one said, "Yes, Iya."

"Are you one of the ones who will restore the beauty of the earth?"

A chorus of them responded, "Yes, Iya!"

"Will you make the music and dance?"

"Yes, Iya! Of course, Iya! Indeed, Iya! We will!"

And their beautiful voices were so clear that I stretched my arms to embrace them.

"Well, if there are more of you than there are of them." (I pointed a trembling finger.) "As long as the children of the first, sober making continue to still the hands of the children of My drunkenness, who are not kind, not intelligent, not beautiful in spirit, as long as the children of the first, sober making are willing to do the work, there's no need for me to destroy the earth."

Are *you* a child of the first, sober making? If you are, in the blank below, write, "Yes, Iya." And if there are enough of you, I won't have to destroy anything.

So, I think I'll have another drink. *Gulp.*

THE COMING OF IKU

The story of how death came into the world is found in most cultures. Usually, the first death occurs by accident or because of irresponsible behavior.

This story can be found throughout the diaspora. Often, the messenger is an animal such as a mouse, a turtle, or a spider.

In the beginning, Iku, Death, did not exist on Earth. He lived with Olodumare. But Iku was not satisfied with His lot. He wanted to go into the other dimension. So, He pleaded and pleaded with the deities until, at last, They coerced Olodumare into allowing Death to go into the world of the humans.

The humans, meanwhile, were under the impression that they were entitled to eternal life. Had God made a promise, or were humans assuming too much?

With Death now among the humans, Damballah suggested that the deities send humans new skins to wear when their bodies grew old and cold. These skins could be renewed in cycles of divine order. Damballah put the new skins into a basket and asked Aja, the dog of heaven, to take it to the human family.

On the way, Aja became very hungry. Fortunately, He met bush rat, turtle, and some other animals who were having a feast. He was invited to join them and satisfy His hunger. When His belly was full, He lay in the shade of an iroko tree to rest.

While He was resting there, Python approached Him and asked Him what was in the basket. Aja replied that He was carrying skins to humans, and then He went back to sleep.

Python waited in the bush until he was sure that Aja was fast asleep. Then he slipped over to the basket and opened it. Inside he saw the most beautiful skins! So many colors! He took the basket and slid silently away into the bush.

Soon afterwards, Aja woke and discovered that Python had stolen the basket of skins. He ran as fast as He could to tell the humans what had happened.

The humans were beside themselves. How could this happen? What did this mean? They demanded that the skins be returned to them. But who, oh, who could they appeal to?

The humans spoke with the water and the trees; they pleaded with the wind and the thunder—they even yelled at the sun and the moon and shook their fists at the heavens high above.

But Olodumare did not respond. Damballah, the rainbow serpent, was the one who made man understand that the lost skins could not be given to humans again.

It all simply meant that Iku could come to visit, that humans would have to die when they became old. When Death came to call, the humans would simply shed their bodies as the snake does its skin. But from then on, the spirit would live on in new skins, on new days.

Nedra Williams, *Obba*. 2022.

THE OBA'S FEAST

Rediscovering Obba

The goddess Obba is a most important figure in this the story of "The Oba's Feast," the great feast of Shango, the lord of thunder.

It must have been in the early seventies that I was called to audition for a part in a play entitled *Shango de Ima*, written by Pepe Carril. The play was something new for many of us because it attempted to explain the complex relationships between the Orishas according to Cuban culture—and to do that in twenty scenes that transcended time and moved through space from heaven to Earth and back again. The auditions were highly competitive. Everybody in the Bay Area who was interested in Orisha worship, folkloric theater, ceremonial costuming, traditional makeup, oration, and music wanted a part in this production. After many challenges and changes, I was called upon to play Iya Nla,[8] the great mother of creation, a female aspect of Obatala, the King of the White Cloth. You met Iya Nla in "Obatala's Mistake." I was also selected to play my goddess, Oshun, both as a capricious child and as the sensuous woman who seduced Shango, the king.

---

8   Pepe Carril's play uses the name Orishnla to refer to the goddess whom I have been calling Iya Nla in this book.

But most important for me then, and now, was the character known as Obba, the first wife of Shango. In the play's version of the story, Obba was a submissive, quiet, jealous woman who was always in competition with some other woman for Her husband's attention. This characterization is a typically patriarchal telling of Obba's story. According to the old story, Oshun or Oya (or sometimes both) convinced Obba to cut off Her ear and put it into a soup to be served at the Oba's feast. In the play, She is told that putting a "piece of your body" in the soup would make Shango love Her more than any other woman. After all, the key to a man's heart is through his stomach.

Being African American, I saw this directive as a terrible misuse of a folk saying. In Southern Black culture, we compliment a cook by saying, "Girl, you musta put yo foot in this. It sho is good." Was it possible something got lost in diasporic translation, I wondered?

There came a point in the play when Obba serves Shango's most illustrious guests, who discover Her ear floating in the soup and expose the bloody bandage around Her head. Disgusting! How dare She humiliate the king before His guests? In anger Shango beats Obba and sends Her running from the compound streaming tears of blood. And although the playwright named Oshun and Oya as the ones who trick Obba into committing this travesty, They both, along with Yemaya, request a hearing in the court of Iya Nla and demand justice for Obba. In court, Shango is arrogant. He claims that His first wife embarrassed Him and that embarrassment was an attack on His kingdom. He had the right to defend His reputation and His home. In short, He showed no remorse.

Yet, to my shock and dismay, in this script Obba stood up and declared that it was all right for Shango to abuse Her if He continued to love Her. Unfortunately, this version was the most popular and, for many years, the only story one could hear about Obba.

This story sent me into a rage that lasted for twenty years.

I spent decades being disgusted as I searched for an alternative to this story, which was sometimes cited (by diviners) as a preordained justification for domestic violence! My search included comparing the beliefs and sayings of New Orleans and some of the Caribbean islands. There are similarities such as "The rooster controls the hen house" or "He beats you 'cause he loves you." This kind of "love" is dangerous.

Further investigation led me to a Cuban description of Obba as the "Orisha of commerce and submission." What the hell did that mean? I could not fathom what those two things had to do with each other. So, I kept looking until I found a Brazilian image of Her wearing a pink Marie Antoinette-type dress with a ball and chain on Her ankle, and She was crying tears of blood. Submission and commerce. I thought of Her as an expression of the sorrow of the African woman as she lost her children and her freedom in the slave trade.

In the seventies, I traveled in circles of women who were also seeking deeper definitions of the goddesses of the world. We were not satisfied with "Nobody, the wife of Somebody" or simply "fertility artifact." We wanted to know the true identities and roles of the goddesses and what They meant in our lives.

So, I asked my colleagues to please meditate on Obba, to seek Her out in dreams, and to discuss the meaning of Her in our collective consciousness. I am so grateful to Max Dashu for her decades of work, which offered us a whole library of deities, helping me to understand Obba in a global context.[9] We found that in several cultures, one could find a goddess (such as Hera, the jealous wife of Zeus the playboy, or Persephone, the rape survivor) who was exploited by Her man and who then blamed and tricked other women instead of blaming Her abuser. The popular anthologies always presented these as stories of female jealousy, rivalry, failure, and destruction. Women's disempowerment was the chosen perspective of patriarchal interpretations of myth and folklore.

Every time I came upon the bloody ear soup story, I prayed and looked for something else. After decades of searching (it was the early nineties now), I had an occasion to attend a kariocha (initiation) in San Francisco. A businesswoman who was being initiated for Oshun also received Obba. In the ceremony, this initiate was given a necklace of rose quartz and clear crystal. I surmised the rose quartz was for compassion and clear quartz for clarity—two stones associated with Oshun. But the initiate also received a gold anvil with several smithing tools. And I realized that Obba is a goldsmith! Again, I was reminded of the Gold Coast of West Africa and the pain and sorrow of the slave trade.

Then, one fine day in the late nineties, I attended a lecture at the Museum of the African Diaspora in San Francisco. Maestra Bobi Céspedes,[10] an honored elder priest-

---

9   https://www.suppressedhistories.net/

10   https://www.bobicespedes.com/index.php/about

ess of Obatala knowledgeable in the music and folklore of Cuba, delivered a talk that described an empowered and revered Obba, based on conversations with older Cuban *madrinas*. I am grateful to her for opening my ears. Once you remove the foot of colonial patriarchy crushing your neck, you can breathe, and a wide range of perspectives, emotions, and possibilities can be ingested, digested, and absorbed into your understanding of reality.

The tragic mutilation story occurs in Oyo, the town sacred to Shango. But in Africa, Obba's home village is Ogbomosho. There, the story of Her victimization does not exist. Upon learning this, I remembered the traditions of "patrifocal" marriages, in which the wives leave their village and take up residence in the domicile of their husbands. In these cases, the women are removed from the protection and recognition of their natal family. They are then subject to the rules and regulations of the husband's village, where they may become strangers in a strange land.

Oshun's hometown is Oshogbo. There She is highly revered as an independent woman with wealth, status, and the freedom to choose Her lovers. She does not fight over men; men fight over Her.

In this story, three characters from three different towns, Oshogbo, Ogbomosho, and Oyo—and with three different sets of customs, attitudes, etc.—come together. What's more, I realized that the Obba River is the main tributary of the Oshun River. They dance *together* in a series of rapids. Further, Oya is associated with the Niger River, which flows some one hundred and fifty miles from the Oshun and Obba Rivers, with all three emptying at the Atlantic coast.

When we turn to nature for our interpretation of the orature, what we find is *a confluence of the feminine waters*. Not a conflict between three women.

Later, I was blessed to speak with Cuban and African American priests who'd attended shrines, recited prayers, and received blessings from Obba. They told me that She is a beautiful mother and that She and Oshun are friends.

In my rendition of "The Oba's Feast," I have presented Obba as a multidimensional woman, based on what I've gleaned of Her over my years of discovery. We see Her as the devoted wife and as a disciplined domestic goddess. She bravely forages in the wilds in search of food and medicine. She acts as a liberator, then takes Her place as one of a trio of goddesses with jurisdiction over burial customs and the cemetery.

Seeing Her fullness has relieved me of my disgust and redirected my rage. I now see Obba as the defender and protector of oppressed women.

Now, let us attend "The Oba's Feast." Our reservations are confirmed.

So Bold a Thief

Every dignitary in the country was invited to the eloquent feast. They would come from every direction, traveling many miles for days to arrive dressed in their finest garbs with an entourage of servants, wives, and children. The village was buzzing with excitement in anticipation of the arrival of these distinguished guests who brought exotic spices, finely woven cloth, precious jewelry, and stimulating entertainment. The food, the music, and the magic of it was sure to be enjoyed by all.

The great hall of Shango's compound was decorated with palm fronds, ashoké[11] cloth, glittering beads, and cowries. The musicians sat in a corner of the hall surrounded by Batá drums,[12] shekeres,[13] and agogô bells,[14] awaiting the moment when they would play the processional music for the arrival of Shango's father, Obatala.

As Shango extended His hand to welcome the first of His guests, there was the sound of gunfire outside the great hall. His two faithful soldiers Timi and Gbonka came running into the compound.

---

11   Ashoké (aso oke) means "top cloth." It is the most prestigious handwoven cloth in Yoruba couture. Complete ashoké outfits are worn during important religious ceremonies and social engagements.

12   The Batá are the sacred drums played at important ceremonies. A battery consists of three double-headed drums that are shaped like an hourglass. One end is larger than the other. They are the Iya (Mother), Okonkolo (Father), and the Itotoli (Child). They speak the language of the ancestors and the deities in highly specialized rhythms and songs. They originate in Oyo (Nigeria) but are played throughout the diaspora.

13   The shekere (from Yoruba "Ṣẹ̀kẹ̀rẹ̀") is a dried calabash with beads or cowries woven into a net covering the gourd. They are usually of three sizes. They are played by shaking the beads while striking the bottom with the hands. Some shekere players juggle the gourds and dance while playing them.

14   An agogô bell is usually made of metal (iron) and played with a wooden stick. The instrument may be a single elongated bell or two bells attached to each other. They are played with the Batá drum and the shekere at important events.

They lowered their eyes and slightly bent their knees as they addressed Him: "Kawo Kabeyesi."[15]

Shango granted them the right to speak.

"A thief entered Your stable and stole Your favorite horse," Timi reported.

"Yes, Kabeyesi, he was wounded by one of the guards, but he rode off," Gbonka added.

"He escaped?" Shango asked, a glower creeping over His face.

"Yes, Kabeyesi," they answered in unison.

Then Shango commanded, "The two of you must catch this thief and throw him in the pit. Let nothing disturb my feast today. You understand?"

They both responded, "Yes, Kabeyesi," and with that they mounted their horses and rode out to track down the thief.

Obatala's Journey

Obatala, the King of the White Cloth, consulted[16] the Babalawo,[17] as is the custom for all important events. Together They sat on the mat and began to pray:

---

15   The traditional greeting before Shango. The name comes from a Yoruba title for a chieftain and can be translated as "He who cannot be questioned." Devotees rise from their seats when His name is called and lower their eyes in His presence.

16   Ifa divination, the process of consulting ikin or opele to discern the messages from the ancestors and the Orishas. The meaning is revealed through 256 Odus. Each Odu contains proverbs, myths, and folktales that make predictions for the seeker and provides prescriptions to bring balance into the person's life.

17   Father of secrets, the title given to the priest who is adept at reading the Ifa oracle.

"Ibache[18] *Olofin, Olorun, Olodumare.*[19]
Ibache Orunmila,[20] *Elerin Ipin . . ."*[21]

The diviner chanted to open the portal between heaven and Earth. He counted all the ikin,[22] and the opele[23] fell heavily on the divining tray.

After a moment of silence, the Babalawo spoke. "You need to make a sacrifice. Bring Ifa a length of white cloth, a gourd of palm oil . . ."

Obatala said, "Sacrifice?"

The Babalawo continued: ". . . a skin of palm wine . . ."

Obatala shook His head. "Why should I make a sacrifice?"

The Babalawo continued: ". . . and sixteen cowries."

"I'm going to My own Son's feast!"

"You need to make a sacrifice."

"But I have done nothing wrong!" Obatala exclaimed.

"As You wish," the Babalawo said as he cleared the divining tray and rose from the mat.

Obatala bid him "odabo"[24] and walked over to His grooming station. There He oiled His black skin with shea butter, trimmed His beard, and placed a crown with an emblem of the sun on His head of bushy gray hair. His luminous white agbada[25] was embroidered with stars.

---

18   A salutation that expresses respect for the power of the spirit.

19   The sun, the sky, the universe.

20   The prophet who illuminated the wisdom of the Ifa oracle.

21   "Respect to the prophet, the witness to creation."

22   Palm nuts used in Ifa divination.

23   The divining chain used in Ifa divination.

24   A respectful way to say "goodbye."

25   An elaborately embroidered robe made of ashoké and other precious fabrics to indicate the stature of the wearer.

Then He tucked His whip into the saddle and mounted His fine white stallion. As He rode leisurely out of the compound, the men of the village threw cowrie shells on the path before Him, the women covered their heads in respect, and the children stepped out of His way. Sauntering out of the village, His horse pranced along the bank of the Oshun River, and Obatala imagined Himself making a grand entrance into the palace of His son, the Alaafin[26] of the mighty city of Oyo.

Only a few miles before He reached the entrance to the city property, Elegba, the Trickster, met Him in the crossroads.

Elegba greeted the old man but did not bow as was the custom. "Alafia,[27] Baba," He said. "How are things with you today?"

"The sun is shining brightly today," Obatala responded as He lifted His chin to the sky.

Elegba touched the horse and smiled. He queried, "Where are you going, Baba?"

Proudly, Obatala responded, "I'm going to the palace of My son, Shango, for there is a great feast in My honor today."

"Indeed?" Elegba grunted. "I wasn't informed." He rolled His eyes and then "accidently" stepped on the horse's foot. The steed took a step back. "Ah, Baba, there is a thorn in Your horse's hoof," He said, with what sounded like concern filling His voice. "Let Me pull it out."

---

26   Alaafin, or The Owner of the Palace, is the title of the political leader of Oyo. The legendary man Shango was the fourth Alaafin of Oyo.

27   A greeting wishing the person peace and good health.

When Elegba bent over, He slipped a small gourd of red palm oil out of His pouch. He put the oil on His hands and rubbed the horse's foot. Then He stroked its side, His stained hands brushing Obatala's robe. "There, that's better," Elegba concluded.

"Come with Me to the feast," Obatala offered.

But Elegba declined. "Thank you for Your kind offer, Baba. But I have another important engagement."

"What could be so important, Elegba?" the old man asked.

Elegba narrowed His eyes. "I'm going to wrestle with Iku[28] today!" He exclaimed.

"You plan to wrestle with Death?" Obatala asked, incredulous.

"And I will win!" Elegba declared.

"Be advised, young man," Obatala admonished as He stroked His beard. "No one can take life from Death."

"Ah yes, Baba: perchance, I am the No One Who Can."

Obatala chuckled and shook His head.

"Beware, old man! There are bandits on the road," Elegba warned as Obatala rode off toward Oyo.

Fare Fit for a Feast

Meanwhile, the cookhouse of the compound was buzzing with activity.

Oya pranced in carrying Her blood-stained machete. "The hunt was easy today," She announced. "I simply wres-

---

28   Death. He appears as the shadow of the living and brings an end to life as His duty.

tled with Ogun and took what He was unwilling to give."
She slammed a side of bush cow on the table and started
rubbing it with spices.

Yemaya shook Her head. "So, you have been wrestling
with Ogun again?" She teased as She placed a large tray of
akara[29] beside the bloody meat.

"Yes," Oya responded. "It's one of my favorite pastimes."
She turned Her attention to piercing the meat and threw it
into the open flame to cook.

The sound of tinkling bells and a fragrance filled the
room as Oshun danced in, balancing a large calabash on
Her head. "The spices in the market were really fresh today."
She removed the calabash of custard from Her head. As
She lowered it, honey spilled onto everything else on the
table. Meanwhile Yemaya basted Oya's meat with its own
juices and wiped Her hands on Her apron.

The air in the room stood still as Yemaya, Oya, and Oshun looked over the table and awaited the inspection of
Obba, who had quietly entered the cookhouse amidst the
other women's activity.

"And what are you cooking today?" Oshun asked Obba,
eyeing the first wife's simple muslin garb.

"I'm not sure what to cook," She admitted. "Shango is
seldom pleased no matter what dish I prepare."

"Really?" Oshun asked. "What have you cooked for Him?"

The three women shifted in their shoes and waited for
Obba to answer.

Obba said, "I cooked amala."[30]

---

29   A beancake favored by the ancestors.
30   A porridge made with ground corn, okra, and palm oil, said
to be Shango's favorite meal.

"And He didn't like it?" Oya questioned.

"And I made fufu," Obba added.[31]

"But fufu is so easy to make," Yemaya commented.

"He didn't like it," Obba responded.

"How unfortunate," Oshun said. She dripped honey on a beancake, placed it in Her mouth, and licked Her lips.

"We have many guests coming today," Obba said as She scrutinized the food on the table. "I'm afraid we might not have enough food."

"I've caught the meat, I'm cooking the meat, and that's all I'm doing today," Oya announced, moving toward the exit.

The bells on Oshun's ankles played the rhythm of Her hips as She danced around the table, humming.

"Oshun, behave," Yemaya chuckled as She, too, flowed toward the door.

And the three women sauntered out of the kitchen

Obba lingered, critiquing the table. She saw meat, and sweets, and bread. "This meal needs a soup," She mumbled to Herself.

So, She picked up Her foraging calabash and headed for the forest in search of the ingredients to make a savory soup.

Stop, Thief!

Obatala galloped toward Oyo. He expected to arrive just in time to make a grand entrance into Shango's palace. In His head, He could already hear the drums, the shekeres, and

---

31   A starch made of pounded yam or semolina. It is served with a spicy soup and eaten with the fingers.

the agogô bells playing as the chorus sang, "*Ekabo s'ile wa Baba. Ekabo s'ile wa.*"[32]

And because of the song in His head, He could not hear Timi and Gbonka shouting, "Stop, thief!" as they galloped after the man on the white horse with the stain of fresh blood on His robe.

Timi moved faster to ride alongside the supposed thief. Gbonka came up behind and struck the horse with his whip.

There are bandits on the road today, Baba. Obatala remembered Elegba's warning. He rode harder now and fought to beat off the bandits, swinging His horsehair switch.

Timi received a slap across his face and screamed. Gbonka delivered a blow across Obatala's back. Obatala pulled the rein on His horse, making the animal rear up on its hind legs. Obatala's crown fell to the ground and rolled into the bush.

At that moment, Gbonka's whip gripped Obatala's neck and pulled Him off His horse. The old man fell to the ground headfirst and was knocked out cold.

Now they took the old "thief," bruised and bloody, and tied Him up in His dirty gown. They threw His body across the back of the horse and rode quietly off the path, deep into the forest, where they bound Him in a cave at the foot of the mountain.

They cleaned the blood and dirt from that fine horse of Shango's, gave it water to drink, and left it to rest in the rear of the compound. Then they washed their own bodies, dressed in their finest uniforms, and headed for the feast, congratulating each other for a job well done.

---

32   "Welcome to this place." An invitation to join a sacred event.

The Guests Arrive

In preparation for the feast, Oya tied Her palm frond skirt over multi-colored, wide-legged pants and placed a buffalo hide belt around Her waist and a necklace made of stripped beads with nine small copper masks around Her neck.

Yemaya, being the queen mother, chose a flowing gown in seven shades of blue and silver. Necklaces of polished fish scales and coral beads rested gently on Her large angular breasts.

Oshun appeared in the dressing room wearing five yellow silk scarves, five brass bracelets, and a crown of parrot feathers. The tinkling bells on Her hips and Her feet filled the room with music.

The women helped each other to dress Their hair and paint Their faces.

Through it all, Obba was nowhere to be seen.

The main room of the compound was lavishly decorated for the feast. Handwoven palm mats lay on the floors, surrounded by pillows covered in pure white goat skin. Shango's throne was carved from a single branch of the iroko tree. The armrests were ram's horns, and the skin of a leopard rested at His feet. The Oba's crown was embroidered with bright red beads and cowrie shells. He wore a robe of finely woven ashoké cloth and bracelets of Ghanaian gold.

The dignitaries began to arrive. They came from every direction, bringing gifts of finely woven cloth and jewelry made of brass, bronze, ivory, and gold.

Timi and Gbonka greeted each of them with a slight bow, the appropriate handshake, and a small gourd of palm wine. Each dignitary was led to their place of honor around the royal palm mat. The room buzzed with murmured greetings, measured conversation, and compliments to the Oba in clear, loud voices.

Aromas of roasted meat, syrupy sweets, and tropical flowers filled the room as Yemaya, Oya, and Oshun entered to the music of the jewelry They wore. The women placed Their foodstuffs on the mat and took Their places on pillows beside Shango's throne.

As Shango looked around the room, it seemed as if everybody in the world was there—but with two exceptions. The pillow of His wife Obba was pushed aside and vacant. And, more importantly, the finely carved stool He'd reserved for His father, Obatala, sat conspicuously empty. According to custom, the blessing of the elder was needed to start the feast.

At first, everyone was content to sip their palm wine and chuckle at each other's jokes. Yemaya refilled their cups several times. But time passed, and Obatala's seat remained empty.

Oshun recited the menu to entice the appetites of the guests. "Well, let's see what We have here!" She pointed toward Oya's bush cow ribs dripping with spicy cinnamon pepper sauce. And She swirled one of Yemaya's beancakes in the gourd of custard as golden honey dripped from its crust. The guests began to lick their lips, and they heard their stomachs growl.

Oya leaned over to Shango and whispered, "Go ahead and start the feast. You are the king, you know."

A Forest Bargain

Obba placed Her feet carefully upon the forest floor, looking for wild herbs and hardy greens to supplement the food for the celebration. She pinched a leaf or two from several bushes and even plucked flowers to grace the table. But nothing suitable as a contribution to the feast caught Her eye.

She spoke to the forest, asking, "What have you for my soup?"

Without warning, a dwarf sprang up from the trunk of a fallen tree. "Hey, what'd You say?" the dwarf shouted, startling Obba.

Obba studied this creature of the forest. He had one eye, one ear, one hand, and one leg. "Who are You?" She asked.

"I am Osain, the keeper of the plants in the Forest of Forever. Who are You?"

"I am Obba, the wife of Shango."

"Oh, I see," said the dwarf. "What are You doing in My forest?"

Before She could answer, He began to dance around Obba, singing, "*Osain Ade,*[33] *Ashede,*[34] *A ko ko.*"[35] He hopped on His one leg, shook His shoulders, and waved His arm vigorously as He sang.

In spite Her of urgency, Obba found Herself dancing with this funny little man. They danced to exhaustion before falling on the forest floor, laughing.

When Obba caught Her breath, She said, "I'm here looking for a secret ingredient to make a fine soup."

---

33   A crown establishing rank.

34   A recognition that one has power.

35   A vessel that holds power objects.

"Speak a little louder," Osain shouted.

She repeated Herself directly into His singular ear. "I need something for My soup."

The little man led the woman through the bush to a decaying tree trunk. There on the bark was a cluster of wood ear mushrooms.

Osain began to boast. "Here, Obba, is the wood ear mushroom. It is one of the finest in the forest. It is rich in iron and good for the blood and the heart. You should cook it in red palm oil and any other flavoring You want to put in the soup. When it is cooked, it turns a beautiful brown color much like your skin. Do You want some?" He asked.

"Oh yes, please," Obba answered, eyeing the ruffled fungi that crept along the fallen trunk in ear-shaped formations.

"This soup is sure to be the highlight of the meal," said Osain. "But are You willing to pay the price for taking this mushroom out of My forest?"

"Yes," Obba exclaimed, "I'll give anything for it. What do You require?"

Osain broke a thorn from the leopard's claw bush, detached the largest mushroom from the tree trunk, and gave it to Obba.

Then He said, "In return, You must sacrifice a piece of Your body," as He removed the gele[36] from Obba's head.

---

36   A woman's headdress. It is usually made of multicolored cloth and is tied in a style that signifies the woman's position in the culture.

A Stimulating Evening

Despite the absence of His father and first wife, the Oba knew it was time to begin.

But just as Shango raised His hand to start the feast, a figure appeared in the doorway, laughing. Everyone looked to see who it was, but in an instant the figure was gone. When Their gaze returned to the center of the room, there was Obba standing behind Shango. She wore a dress and a gele of plain white muslin fabric with a single strand of pink beads around Her head, neck, and waist.

Proudly, She placed a huge calabash and a ladle in the center of the mat and took Her seat on the pillow behind Shango, who barely noticed Her.

"Let the feast begin," He declared. And with that command, the great Batá drums sounded, the agogô bells accented the rhythm, and the shekeres hummed beneath the bells. Yet Obatala's seat remained empty.

After a gourd of meat and sweets was set aside to feed the spirit of the ancestors, the guests leaned toward the large calabash in the center of the mat. When Obba lifted the cover of the calabash, an enticing aroma floated across the space. She dipped the ladle into the broth and brought forth the *pièce de résistance*, a gigantic wood ear mushroom.

One of the guests gasped. Another shrieked. Yet another held her mouth and belly at the sight of the ear hanging from the ladle.

Shango could not fathom what had caused such an uproar among His distinguished guests—not until His eyes landed on the sight of the ear in the ladle and the blood staining Obba's gele.

"What is this?" He thundered, hovering over Obba.

"It's something I made especially for Your feast, Kabeyesi," She said, attempting to smile. "I thought it would please Your guests."

"You thought to please Me—this, to please Me? It does not please Me!" He leaned over Her menacingly. "Are you trying to poison My guests?" He looked around the room. "Or did You come here simply to embarrass Me?"

Then He raised a hand as if about to strike Her.

"Get out of my face.

"Get out of my compound.

"Get out of my village."

He kicked the calabash of soup, spilling it all over the mat.

As Obba ran out of the room in shame, a great noise rumbled outside. Shango's guests ran to the door to see what it was all about.

There in the crossroads stood Elegba and Iku, ready to fight. The village spectators made a semicircle around Them, which the esteemed guests of the feast joined. The humans watched Elegba closely, while the Ajogun[37] cheered for Iku.

The two began engaging in gidigbo:[38] first Elegba struck out at Iku with His crooked stick. Iku dodged the blow and then slapped Elegba's face. Elegba countered with a roundhouse kick, but Iku grabbed His leg and brought Them both to the ground.

---

37   The eight major (and two hundred minor) negative forces intent on disrupting the progress of humans.

38   A West African martial art that requires courage and spiritual discipline.

This wrestling match went on for a quite a long time. Eventually, the spectators lost interest in the outcome. "No one can take life from Death," they commented, "not even the Trickster."

Elegba countered, "Ah, but I am the only One Who is No One and Everyone at once."

Still, the people returned to their daily business.

Inside the compound, Shango's guests thanked Him for a "stimulating evening" and departed with whispers about His impending demise, given the occurrence of the match and Iku's victory. Surely Death would come to someone soon.

Guests gone, the king sat on His throne, seething with anger. He dismissed His faithful guards, Timi and Gbonka. Only once He was alone with His embarrassment did Shango cry.

As the sun went down, Obatala's seat remained unfilled.

The Daughters of the Gelefun

Yemaya, Oya, and Oshun retired to their quarters. They wrapped Their heads with the Gelefun,[39] the cloth of power, and decided what must be done.

Yemaya spoke first. "This is my fault. I made Shango marry Obba to establish a diplomatic relationship with Ogbomosho. She did Her best, but I can see now that it's not going to work." Yemaya went to chastise Shango and tell Him to go lie down while She cleaned the mat and extinguished the lamps in the main hall.

---

39   An elaborate white "cloth of power" worn by women in positions of authority.

Oshun promised to find Obba and to console Her because "everybody deserves somebody's love."

"When you find Her, I'll provide a permanent place of honor for Her," Oya declared.

Obba left the village with little more than the clothes on Her back, those and a bundle of firesticks, some dried snails, a pot, and bandages for Her wound. She wandered in a daze, unable to comprehend what had just happened. She thought She'd done everything right.

When Osain had cut off Obba's ear, He gave it to the tree to compensate for taking the mushroom. She'd made the sacrifice willingly, and She'd only thought of enhancing the feast as She stirred the soup. Confused, She wandered in the woods, dripping blood and crying.

As sunset yielded to night, Obba heard the echo of moaning in the mountain. Following the sound, She came upon an opening, a cave. There She found an old, black man in dirty white clothes, stained with palm oil and blood. She touched the wound on the back of His head. When the old man rolled over and looked into Her eyes, She recognized Him.

"Baba!" She gasped, lowering Her head.

Obba tended Obatala's wounds with the local herbs She'd gathered; She cooked the snails and fed Him. During the meal, She explained that Shango had exiled Her from the feast. Obatala explained that Shango's guards had attacked Him on the road. They both held Their heads and tried to figure out what went wrong.

Obatala admitted, sheepishly, that He had failed to make the offering to Ifa as the Babalawo instructed. Then He recounted His battle with the "two bandits" Elegba warned Him about.

"Aha," Obba concluded. "Shango failed to invite Elegba to the feast. A grave mistake. There is bound to be chaos everywhere!"

Obba gathered some water from a nearby spring and washed the king's white cloth. Meanwhile Obatala took a handful of soil from the forest floor and fashioned a new ear for His daughter-in-law.

They slept soundly through the night.

When the sun rose, Obba wrapped Her newly healed head.

Obatala dressed in His luminous white cloth. Then He continued His journey to Oyo as Obba walked in the other direction, along the riverbank, to return to Her home in Ogbomosho.[40]

Meanwhile, Oshun also walked along the banks of Her river, searching for Obba. After a time, She found Her sitting at the place of confluence between Their two waters.

Oshun joined Obba on the ground, and They wiggled Their toes in the rapids.

Obba said sadly, "I can see now that Shango will never be the husband I want. I guess I'll just have to live with that."

In turn, Oshun explained that She had learned to live with the constant absence of Her own husband, Orunmila.

---

40   Also Ògbómọ̀ṣọ́: Obba's hometown. A city upriver from Oyo known for agriculture and trading.

"He is the elerin ipin, the chief diviner, the witness to creation. He travels from town to town serving others. I often divine for the local people. He is never at home. And I have many suitors. So, I take other lovers in His absence."

Obba, conversely, committed Herself to a life of celibacy.

Finally, Oya found the two of Them sitting there talking, and She added, "I am the lightning that precedes Shango's thunder in a storm. I'll always outwit Him, and He will always need Me. Obba, I know someone who needs somebody attentive and careful like You."

Oshun adorned Obba's gele with parrot feathers and cowrie shells. "Obba, You are a queen!" she declared.

Oya gave Her a sword and a buffalo hide whip and pronounced, "Obba, You are a warrior."

Then They escorted Her to the cemetery to live with Yewa.[41]

Making Ebbo[42]

The Ajogun, empowered by Iku's victory over Elegba, were running rampant by the time Obatala arrived at the gate of the town.

The first Ajogun to sense Obatala's presence was Confusion, whose retreat began to relieve the people of their bewilderment. Disease took flight, and Paralysis released the hands of the workers. Problems and Loss decided to take a hike, while Curse was exposed as a fraud. Slowly,

---

41   An angel of the night, She is a mortician who lives in the cemetery and oils the body of the dead.

42   A prescribed offering or ritual to reestablish balance in one's life.

Obatala unlocked the gates of Imprisonment and set the people free.

The people clapped, stomped their feet, played drums, and rang bells as they joyfully chanted, "*Maferefun,*[43] *Obatala. Modupe,*[44] *Baba O.*"

Shango descended from His throne and walked out of the palace to see what all the celebration was about. When Shango saw the shining face of His father, dressed in luminous white robes, He prostrated before Him. "*Oba wa to. Orisha obi oso. Dide.*"[45]

Obatala blessed His son and lifted Him up. They spoke in soft tones. Shango explained that a thief had stolen His white horse. Obatala explained that He had been attacked on the road and His horse was confiscated. They surmised that Elegba had smeared palm oil on Obatala's robes and had sent the true thief to steal Shango's horse from the royal stable.

"But, Baba, I know my soldiers are swift and strong enough to dispatch a suspected thief. Who helped you to recover and arrive here today?"

"Why, Your wife did, My son—Obba, Your first, most humble wife."

Shango had no option but to avoid His father's pointed gaze.

So the two of Them went and questioned Elegba. "Who stole the horses? Who smeared palm oil to look like blood? Who brought a fight to the feasts?"

---

43   An expression of gratitude.

44   "Thank you."

45   "Royal one who has fallen, the power of the Orisha lifts you up." A blessing.

With each question Elegba simply smiled and answered, "No One."

Without hesitation, the father and son gathered up offerings of cowrie shells, palm oil, cloth, and parrot feathers and journeyed to the house of the Babalawo to seek divination and make ebbo.

Gail Williams, *Marketplace 2*. 2022.

PART II:
THE COWRIES

THE DIVISION OF THE COWRIES

Ekabo S'ile wa. Welcome, welcome, come on in. Enter the African marketplace, a place of plenty.

Here you will find many things: fresh fruits and vegetables, grains, beans, and spices, bananas, rice, pepper, and peas. There are things most people from the U.S. have never seen before. Dried catfish on a stick, smoked bush rat, and yams— and no, I don't mean that yellow-orange sweet potato you love to eat candied or as soup, pudding, and pie. The African yam is covered in skin as coarse as tree bark, scaly and brown on the outside with tough, white fiber on the inside.

The African market is a beautiful place. Here are lots of fabrics, cotton, silk, embroidered lace. You've probably seen those before, but have you touched the finely woven Nigerian ashoké, felt the weight of bogolan mudcloth from Mali, or marveled at the multicolored patterns of kente cloth from Ghana? The jewelry is amazing! Silver, gold, and copper, brass, and ivory too. You'll see bracelets and anklets, hairpins and combs, earrings and finger rings. Most often, you'll see beads made of wood, stone, and bone displayed in gourds and baskets. But you won't see the waist beads that women wear beneath their clothes. They are a secret charm to increase their fertility. You may not recognize the elephant hair bracelets and the strips of buffalo hide that men wear only when they hunt or go to war. Those are secret, too.

As you walk through the market, you'll come to that very special place where medicines are sold. Here you will find bright red parrot feathers, dried chameleon skins, antelope horns, palm oil, and powdered fire ants.

But inside the diviner's hut is where the real magic begins. Here the diviner casts palm nuts and cowrie shells, river stones, and python bones with invocations to open the portal between heaven and Earth. Now the deity's voice is heard; now the ancestors give us the word.

Above all, and everywhere in the marketplace, cowries will be found.

Ejigbomekun Market in Ile-Ife, Nigeria, is the most famous market in the African world. People come from all over the continent to shop there. Some come from as far away as the Americas, the Caribbean, and Europe. This market is known for its beauty, prosperity, and peace ... um, well, most of the time.

At the beginning of time, people wandered around the earth, hunting, and gathering to find food. Then Orisha Oko created agriculture. He identified the foods that lived in the bush and gathered them. He invented the plow and taught the people how to plant those wild foods in the year-round farm just outside the gates of their village.

This was the beginning of subsistence farming.

Every year the African yams grew bigger and bigger. Some of them grew to the size of a small child.

The people were so grateful for food security that they took a gigantic yam and placed it on the altar. They played drums and sang to the spirit of the yam. They performed this ritual every harvest for years and years and years. The African yam is an original heirloom.

Soon, the people organized markets, centers of commerce where they celebrated their newfound abundance and traded all of the foods and other goods they'd hunted, found, crafted, and grown. And African women were (and remain to this day) the star entrepreneurs of the marketplace.

The Sun was shining bright and hot that morning when the three sisters, Yemaya, Oya, and Oshun, entered the market, fully equipped to set up their stalls. Oya swept the dirt with a long palm broom, making a serpentine symbol on the ground. Yemaya laid a thick sisal mat on top of the symbol. Then She anchored four poles into the corners of the mat and threw a length of dark blue fabric over the top. The cool blue canopy protected them from the sun. Oshun made a table by stacking several crates upon each other, and She opened three canvas folding chairs.

Yemaya stacked Her fabrics, Oshun laid out Her produce, and Oya displayed Her buffalo horns and deer toes. The sisters stood tall and proud as They displayed their wares to those who passed by.

"Ashoké," Yemaya called out as She held up a length of beautiful blue fabric, but the customer just walked on by.

Oshun cooled Herself with a perfumed fan and offered the people free samples of Her honey. But somehow, they declined.

Oya rattled some snake bones and clacked Her buffalo horns together, questioning the crowd, "You need juju? Get it here."

Many people came to Their stall—they looked, touched; some even tasted—but no one bought anything.

The three sisters sat down. The Sun was high in the sky now, the Wind stirred slightly, and a little whirlpool of dust danced past the sisters' stall.

After a while, a man approached Their stall wearing dusty white clothes and a protruding head wrap, leading a goat on a rope.

"Good morning, sisters," the raggedy man greeted Them.

"Good afternoon, sir," They replied in unison.

"I wonder if You three could sell my goat for me?"

The three sisters looked at the man.

"I'll share the profits with you," he continued.

The sisters looked at the goat.

"Sell this goat for twenty cowries," he said. "Hold ten cowries for me and keep the rest for Yourselves."

The three sisters looked at each other. Silently They decided that it was a good deal, and They agreed to sell the man's goat for him.

Then They watched him walk down the path.

After a while, a well-dressed man in a heavily beaded cap approached the sisters' stall.

"Good evening," the man greeted. "What a fine goat. Is it for sale?"

"It is," the sisters responded.

"How much?" the man inquired.

They told him, "Twenty cowries."

The man paid Them gladly from his petty cash pouch and strolled off, pulling the goat behind him.

Yemaya counted out ten cowries and set them aside for the goat man. Then She divided the cowries for Herself and Her sisters. "Here's one, two, three cowries for me; one, two, three cowries for Oya; and one, two, three cowries for Oshun. Ah, and there's one cowrie left. Well, I should get that cowrie because I'm the oldest."

The other sisters disagreed. Just then a young boy in a blue cap stopped to look at some fabric.

Yemaya approached the child and said, "Little one, in the division of the cowries, don't you think that She Who is the eldest should have the extra cowrie?"

"Yes, Mother," the boy agreed.

Oshun sent the child on his way and gathered up all the cowries. "Now let's try this again," She said. "Here's one, two, three cowries for Yemaya; one, two, three cowries for Oya; and one, two, three cowries for me. And there's one cowrie left. Of course, it's Mine."

Just then, Oshun turned around and saw a handsome young man in a red hat, inhaling the scent of Her spices. She dipped Her finger in some honey and rolled it across his lips. "Now, tell Us truly, in the division of the cowries, She who is the youngest should have the extra cowrie, yes?"

The young man licked his lips and said, "Whatever You want, honey. Whatever You want."

Oya stepped in. "Just a minute," She said as She chased the young man away. "Now look, I'm gonna divide these cowries the right way. Here's one, two, three cowries for Yemaya; one, two, three cowries for Oshun; and one, two, three cowries for me."

"What about the extra cowrie?" Oshun asked with an attitude.

Oya spotted an ancient man wearing a black hat creeping along past their stall. She called him over and said,

"Now listen, mister, you know and I know that in the division of the cowries, it is the middle sister who receives the extra cowrie, right?"

The old man shook his head and declared that he just couldn't remember, and he walked on.

Over and over the sisters counted the cowries one, two, three. Over and over, there was one cowrie left. Yemaya accused Oya of being disrespectful. Oya declared it was silly of Oshun to think that She deserved the extra cowrie, and Oshun laughed in Oya's face. Soon Their voices disturbed the peace of the marketplace.

As the Sun was going down, the goat man returned. "Ah, you've sold my goat."

"Indeed," Yemaya said.

"Here's your money," Oshun said, handing him his ten cowries.

"But there's a dispute," Oya spat out.

"A dispute?" the goat man questioned. "Why is there a dispute?"

Oya explained. "Every time We count out the cowries, We have one, two, three for Yemaya; one, two, three for Oshun; and one, two, three for Me with one cowrie left. We can't decide Who should get the extra cowrie."

The goat man laughed. "No wonder there's a dispute! Have You forgotten the custom of First Cowrie? On any day of good fortune in the marketplace, we should throw the First Cowrie on the path for those whose crops failed."

The sisters dropped Their heads in shame and threw the First Cowrie on to the path.

Then They lifted Their eyes to the sky, and each woman threw Her own three cowries onto the path as well. They let out a sigh of satisfaction, packed up Their wares, and left the marketplace, singing.

As night fell, a mysterious figure wearing a three-colored hat—blue, red, and black—collected the cowries from all the stalls in the marketplace and walked on down the path, laughing.

All things begin and end with Elegba.

ELEGBA AND THE TWO FRIENDS

Elegba has often been called "the Trickster"—but this is a misnomer that insinuates He is merely a clown. On the contrary, Elegba is the master of the crossroads: trickery is His power, not His fault. He is seen as both a mischievous child and an ancient wise man. He brings order out of chaos and dissolves it into pure potential again.

He has several very important functions:

He is a magician. He spins the wheel of fortune so that the elements of earth, air, fire, and water come together in myriad ways to create new perceptions of reality.

He is the linguist. All ceremonies begin and end with Him. He translates the language of humans into that of the gods. When humans speak to the forces of nature, He translates our human language into that of the deities, delivers our prayers, and allows us to understand meaning through His interpretation.

He is the enforcer. Human life is conditioned. Many things have already been decided for us by our very nature as humans. We must be born, live, and die. This is destiny. Yet we still have the elements of chance and choice. Chance shows itself when an opportunity arrives to experience something new or different. When several options are placed before us, we make a choice. Often the choices we make are based on our perceptions of "reality." Sometimes we get a chance to change our perception, make a different choice, and change our behavior and the course of our lives.

In this story, two friends encounter Elegba, the Trickster-Magician, who comes between them and tricks them into a shift in perception.

It seems that these two people had grown up together and eventually came to own farms on opposite sides of the road in this little village. They spoke to each other from across the road every day and agreed on things such as the weather, the conditions of the crops, and the market value of their wares.

One day they noticed a little man wearing a funny hat walking from east to west on the road between them. One of the friends commented about the man wearing the funny red hat, and the other said the hat was black. They each shrugged and went on about their work.

After a while, they saw the same little man walking east to west on the road between them. This time one of the friends said that he now saw the man's red hat, and the other replied that the hat was certainly blue. They looked askance and couldn't help but wonder what was wrong with the other's eyesight. But they continued their work, nonetheless.

The workday was almost over when again they saw that same little man walking east to west on the road between them.

"Aha!" one said. "I see now the blue hat you spoke of."

But when the other looked, indeed he saw a red hat!

The two friends stood on each side of the road and finally began to argue. They accused each other of being color-blind, slow-witted, dishonest, and even cursed!

Just as they were about to become violent with each other, the little man came walking down the road west to east. He stopped in the place between the two of them, took off His hat, and twirled it on the tip of His finger, laughing as He walked away.

Then they realized that Elegba, the Trickster-Magician, had come to shake up their perceptions of reality and their attitudes toward each other.

Thereafter, the two committed to checking facts before making assumptions and to speaking what they honestly felt about each other. Gradually their relationship changed. By digging deep, planting anew with diligence and care, their relationship matured and, like the yams in their gardens, yielded an abundant harvest.

OGUN'S BUSH KNIFE

This tale of Ogun teaches us that a "blessing" bestowed on us that does not match our authentic nature is really a burden in disguise.

At one time there were no cities in Yorubaland. The land was covered in thick trees, winding vines, and bushes with long, sharp thorns. Wild beasts trampled the open fields, dangerous creatures inhabited the water, and insects with deadly stingers covered everything. The people had no houses, no tools, and no weapons. Sometimes they made traps of branches, hoping to catch prey. But most often, they fell victim to the snare of the leopard.

Then Ogun, who slept with His ear to the earth, had a dream that instructed Him on where to dig to find a precious metal. He followed the message in His dream, and, using nothing but a stick, He dug into the earth until He discovered *iron*. A beam of sunlight struck the clump of metal He held in His hand, and Ogun knew what to do! So, He pounded it and pounded it and shaped it into a bush knife. What a wonderful thing He created! The metal was strong, the blade sharp; the length and weight felt just right.

He used his bush knife to cut down some trees, clear a path, and build houses for people to live in. He planted food and fashioned traps to catch small prey, and He even made musical instruments.

Ogun created material civilization.

Because His work was so good, the people crowned Him king. Ogun accepted His crown, hung it on a tree branch, and walked into the deep woods to spend time with His friends, the bush cow and the lizard.

The people in the village did not see their king for many days and nights. They had no guidance and did not know what to do with themselves. They called out, "Ogun, nibo ni iwo?" ("Ogun, where are you?") They begged, "Oba O, jowo pada wa ba wa!" ("Oh King, please come back to us!") For many nights they cried.

Then, early one morning, a man covered in palm fronds and leopard skins walked out of the bush and into the village.

The people asked, "Who is this man?"

He answered, "I am your king, Ogun."

But the people looked Him up and down in utter disbelief. "Ah, ah, no, no, no! A king cannot dress this way! A king cannot live in the forest with the animals! The king must sit on His throne and remain in the compound!"

In silence, Ogun listened to the people. He thought of His friends, the bush cow and the lizard. He remembered the sound of the birds singing in the trees. He longed to sleep on the forest floor and to feel the sun caressing His neck.

That night in the compound, Ogun slept on the earth, and again His dream told Him what to do.

So, He made hundreds of bush knives and distributed them among the people in the four directions. Then He taught the young men how to forge iron, and He assisted the women with creating beautiful ornaments.

When He was sure that the people could take care of themselves, Ogun left His crown on a staff at the entrance to the village.

Then He disappeared into the thick of the jungle.

When we want to call Ogun, we must play the agogô bell and clang metal against metal. And if you sing loud enough, and call long enough, Ogun just might answer you.

THE FIRST GRAVE

In many of the stories of the African diaspora, Yemaya presents as the Mother of the Orishas, the nurturing mother to humans, and the director of domestic life. She is the ocean, the "saltwater womb of the earth." She is a guardian of women in childbirth and the "sacred portal" through which babies enter the human world. She is Iya Ibeji, the mother of twins, and gives birth to the duality of life.

In this tale, we come to understand that the mother who gives life through the birth canal is also responsible for the grave—the opening in the earth that returns us to the land of the ancestors. This story credits Yemaya as the originator of the Yoruba custom of "second burial." As in other stories, we see the tension between Her as the mother of civilization and Her husband Ogun as the force of wild nature.

At one time Yemaya, the goddess of the ocean, was married to the course fellow Ogun. Ogun was a hard worker, a good provider, and a loving father, but He was, by nature, the wildman in the woods. He was completely lacking in domestic skills. In fact, when He moved through the compound, the pounding of His feet shook the hut and sent

Her clay pots tumbling to the ground. Without effort, He managed to spill Her oils and dyes, almost ruining Her business. And most gravely, He kept His social interactions with the neighbors to a minimum.

Yemaya tried as much as She could to civilize Him, but nothing worked—except for engaging Him in a game of riddles. She'd ask Him, "How does a little man catch a big fish?" He'd answer, "With lots of luck and good bait." Then They'd laugh together. Riddling was great fun, so it became a habit and the only family activity He enjoyed.

But it wasn't enough. One day Yemaya became so frustrated with Him, She just had to get away. But She could not simply walk away: She and Ogun had a beautiful daughter, Odima, and the community of market women truly depended on Yemaya's wisdom and Her skills. After much consideration, Yemaya devised a plan.

She packed up Her best wares and hid them in a bundle under a bush. Then She consumed a small amount of a certain herb and laid Her body down at the foot of a tree. As the evening's sun set over the ocean, Yemaya appeared lethargic. She grew pale, and then Her angular breast stopped dancing.

Odima found Her there beneath the tree and lamented to the people of the village that Iku had taken Her mother. The entire community came together to mourn the loss of this devoted woman, this beloved mother.

Now, in those days, when someone died, their body was washed and oiled and, after a short ceremony, laid across the branches of a great tree. Then the high-flying vultures would descend, pick their bones clean, and carry the people's prayers to the sky.

Well, everyone came to mourn Yemaya. They cried, they moaned, they hugged their heads and bodies, and they tore their clothing. Then they went home to sleep.

After everyone was gone, Yemaya began to recover from the effect of the herb.

She carefully crawled down out of the tree, found Her bundle, and moved Herself to the next town. There She began a new life selling Her wares in the marketplace.

One day, Odima decided to go to market in the next town. Now, this marketplace, Ejigbomekun, was reputed to be the domain of witches. Rumor had it that all kinds of magical things happened there. Time stood still, animals and things talked, and the dead walked alive in this marketplace.

Odima walked through the market. The vendors called out, "Eru, egusi, irigbo, and epau,"[46] naming the seeds, oils, and spices they had for sale. The daughter of water saw a woman who looked a mighty much like Her mother. This woman had Her mother's paisley eyes, full lips, and angular, full breasts.

Odima stood close to the stall of the woman who might be Her mother and quickly rattled off a favorite family riddle. Odima whispered, "A dog has four legs, but . . ."

Without thinking, Yemaya gave the right response: "Can only run one way."

That did it! The daughter was convinced that this woman was indeed Her mother returned from the dead. Odima

---

46   Watermelon seeds, palm oil, hot pepper, and spinach soup spice, respectively.

slipped away quietly and ran home to tell Her father that Her mother was alive in the ghost's marketplace.

Ogun, Who had fallen into a deep depression at the loss of His wife, tried to comfort His daughter and make Her forget this impossible dream. He made iron bracelets and pounded designs in them at His forge. He entertained Her by riding water buffalos and wrestling with leopards. He moved mountains and uprooted trees for Her entertainment—but She did not recover from Her insistence that Her dead mother walked in the land of the living.

Soon Ogun wondered if it really was just the girl's imagination. Reluctantly, He found an excuse to go to the witches' market. As He entered the market, He heard the women call, "Eru, egusi, irigbo, and epau." Among them Ogun spotted a woman who looked a mighty much like His wife. She had His wife's sparkling eyes, Her beautiful figure, and Her flowing, dark, water-like movements.

Quietly, He placed Himself beside the stall of the woman who might be His mate and recited a family riddle: "Why is kindness hard to give away?"

Automatically, Yemaya answered, "Because it keeps coming back," as She had so many times before.

Without a word the wildman picked the woman up, threw Her over His shoulder, and ran out of the marketplace. He ran through the forest, knocking down trees with one hand, crushing bushes beneath His feet, and scattering herds of animals with His frightening cry of outrage. It was not until He reached Their own compound that the wildman slowed His breathing and placed Her on Her feet.

"How can this be?" He asked, bewildered.

Yemaya did not answer Him.

"You ran off. You deserted Me, deserted Our child."

Yemaya turned Her back to Him.

He screamed, "How could You do this?"

This time She turned and looked directly into His eyes. "Why don't You ask Me *why* I did it? Why I left You—why I'd rather be dead?"

By now the entire village was gathered outside His compound, wondering what catastrophe had occurred. When Yemaya came out and showed Herself alive and whole, the community was aghast.

The elders gathered, the Ogboni[47] was called. The diviner invoked all the spirits of creation, poured libations for the ancestors, and consulted the cowrie shells. They sat on the mat and discussed the matter.

The wisest among them spoke. Elegba, the messenger, agreed to interpret it all.

"Ogun's essential nature is His own, and Yemaya's is Her own. In order to keep peace in the village, They must both try to do better in living together among others. So, Yemaya shall became the ruler of the house, and everything inside it shall be as She decides. Ogun shall be the ruler of the land, and everything outside shall be as He decides.

"But because the false death of Yemaya caused so much grief for so many people, we must take precaution so such a thing can never happen again. Therefore, we will no longer wash and oil the body of the dead and leave it for the vultures. From now on, when someone dies, we will dig a deep hole and deposit the body there.

"As all human beings emerge from the sacred portal of woman's body, so too all human beings will return to the

---

47   The High Council of Elders, the Supreme Court.

sacred portal in the belly of the earth. Further, after a year and a day have passed, we shall inquire of the grave again whether this person roams in another town or has gone happily to the land of the ancestors."

Nedra Williams, *Oya*. 2022.

OCHOOSI'S ARROW

When we are in harmony with nature, everything seems to go our way. When things go wrong, we look for someone or something to blame besides ourselves. This is a story of self-sabotage.

Ochoosi was the finest, leanest young man you'd ever want to meet. Blood-filled veins ran just beneath the pecan-colored skin of His long, muscular arms and flowed into His nimble, slender fingers. When He rubbed His chest and belly with red palm oil, as hunters do, those muscles glistened even in the dark. His sculptured legs could sprint like a gazelle, yet He always walked carefully around the plants on the forest floor. He never made a sound!

It was His nature to rise early in the morning, to gather His bows and arrows and to anoint the tips of them with enough poison to paralyze anything they touched instantly. Always sure of His aim, He'd pull His bowstring and watch the arrow soar through the air to pierce the hearts of the wild birds, His favorite prey.

Ochoosi mounted His quiver of arrows, settled his bow along the crest of His shoulder blade, and headed for the door. He stopped to greet His mother, who sat in Her rocking chair listening to the coos and hums of His African grey parrot, His only pet.

"Alafia, Mother." He smiled as He kissed Her on the forehead.

"Alafia, My son," She responded. "Be careful in the forest this morning, Son."

He chuckled a bit. "Don't worry, Mom. The forest and I are friends, remember?" He kept walking.

"The forest was Your father's friend, too," She called after Him, watching Him disappear into the bush. Agbe remembered the days when She and Her husband Odede, the great hunter, had walked the forest together. They would come home with pigeons, geese, and guinea fowl, enough to feed the entire village. Now all She had left of Him was a memory, His son, and Her blue apron.

Ochoosi stepped through the woods, being careful not to crush any plants, crack any twigs, or disturb any insects' nests.

Then, a flutter in the bush! He placed an arrow in His bow and aimed at the thing that moved.

That afternoon, He shot a duck, a hen, a fat goose, and a pigeon, and He brought them all home for His mother to cook. Just like every day, He gave a bit of grain to His only pet as He walked past His mother into the house.

And, just like every day, when He left again, She called behind Him, "Take care, Son."

He smiled reassuringly. "Everything is fine, Mom."

And again, He walked through the forest, crushing nothing, making no sound, and bringing great bounty home.

One evening, at just about sunset, Ochoosi decided to hunt. As He was about to step through the door, His mother pleaded, "Please, Son, don't hunt in the dark!"

Ochoosi simply kissed Her on the forehead.

As He scurried toward the door, His parrot called out, "Beware. Take care. Take care. *Beware!*"

On that evening, when Ochoosi entered the bush, a twig snapped, and a plant cried beneath His feet.

Before the always silent hunter could register this strangeness, *Something* shiny rustled in the bush! Ochoosi shot at it and—to His own shock—missed. That shiny *Something* moved quickly between the trees.

Ochoosi followed it. Each time it moved, Ochoosi followed it. And each time He shot at it, He missed.

As night fell, the plants and the twigs progressed from wordless protest to outright screams. "Don't step on me! Don't step on me!" they cried.

In more ways than one, Ochoosi was lost. So He sat down at the foot of the iroko tree and tried to sleep.

But still, *Something* called out, "Ode Mata, Ode Mata." ("Hunter, don't kill me.") It echoed in His head as He tossed and turned, dreaming through an eternal night in the Forest of Forever.

Finally, the sun rose, and Ochoosi woke up. He could see His own tracks on the forest floor marked by the crushed plants and broken twigs. They led Him back to His mother's house.

But when He arrived, He found her rocking chair empty and parrot feathers all over the floor! He raced through every room asking, "Where is My mother? Where is My parrot?"

He ran through the house and into the backyard, where He found His mother sitting on a log with Her head hanging down.

"Mother, are You all right?" He asked.

His voice startled Her. She rose, blinked Her eyes, and stared at Him.

"Ochoosi, You're alive?" She moved toward Him. "You've been gone so many nights; My son, I feared You were dead."

He led Her by the hand into the house. She moved slowly and seemed to have aged. Ochoosi sat Her down and kissed Her on the forehead. With eyes lowered, He saw the feathers of His only pet scattered on the floor.

"Where is My parrot?" The question filled the room. After a long silence, He answered Himself: "A thief has stolen My bird!"

Agbe lowered Her eyes and said, "Oh, yes, *Something* broke into the house while I was sleeping. *Something* was hungry and took Your bird. I waited many nights for You," She said, almost apologetic, "but you never came."

It outraged Him that a thief had terrorized His mother and stolen His pet. So, He picked up His bow and arrows and stomped through the forest, stepping on plants and twigs every time His feet hit the ground. He relished their cries.

Ochoosi dipped His arrow in the strongest poison He had and lifted it up to the sky. Then He commanded, "Let this arrow land in the heart of the one who killed My parrot. Ashe, ashe O. Make it so. Make it so!"

Once He let that arrow go, it penetrated the canopy, and the forest screamed, "Ode Mata, Ode Mata!"

Having released His anger and trusting that His arrow had found its mark, Ochoosi walked back to His house, calmed.

But when He arrived, He found His mother sitting in Her rocking chair with an arrow in Her heart. She'd feared the forest had taken Him, just as it had taken Odede, His father. And it was She who had been hungry for Her son and Her husband, so She had sacrificed His parrot to feed Her grief.

These stories can really get you in the gut, especially when they come up in a divination for your own life. Walk carefully in the forest and humbly on your spiritual path.

Nedra Williams and Gail Williams, *Warriors*. 2022.

THE DEER WOMAN OF OWO

A Wild Woman in the Woods

This is one of my favorite tales because it is rich with symbolism and lends itself to multiple layers of interpretation. This story is most popular in the town of Owo, where Orunsen is celebrated during the dry season. But in most cultures, shape-shifting creatures are not to be trusted. In the future, I'd like to dedicate an entire book to this tale, for I've explored its depth for many years in many ways.

During the late sixties, I performed this tale at community centers, storytelling festivals, and celebrations of Black culture around the country. In the mid-seventies the players of CommonArts Cultural Center, a cast of seven people, presented this story as a one-act play at La Peña Cultural Center in Berkeley, California. It was warmly received.

Once, in a fit of mad inspiration, I re-scripted and directed this story as a musical dance-drama with a cast of sixty junior high school students (Frances Willard Junior High School, Berkeley, 1980). Ms. Jackie Barnes created the choreography, and Osha Newman, a well-known Bay Area mural artist, designed the sets. The students researched the music, the costumes, the makeup, the culture, and the environment of the story. In our script, the wind whistled, the river sang, and the trees danced. We were a multiracial, multicultural cast. Orunsen was played by an Asian ballerina, Renrengen by a young Black man with strong African features; the drum rhythms were Cuban, and the dance style was Brazilian. When Orunsen died, the dancer did an adagio (a slow fluid motion) off the edge of the stage into the arms of six pallbearers, who moved to a drumbeat slowly up the center aisle of the auditorium, each carrying a candle in one hand. They disappeared through the back door, and the house lights came on for intermission. The audience exhaled, and the room emptied.

Twenty minutes later, the cast reassembled, and we performed the second half of the show. At the end, the resurrected Orunsen threw cowrie shells from a raised platform to the audience in a gesture of generosity. The house lights came on, the cast bowed, and the audience clapped, cheered, and pelted them with rose petals purchased during the intermission. Notes from this performance were filed away in the records of the California Arts Council.

"The Deer Woman of Owo" is the popular version of the sacred Odu Osa-Ogunda. This story is populated by Orunsen, the wildwoman in the Woods, an aspect of Oya, the queen of the winds of change and mother of the marketplace. She is a bush cow, a wild creature of nature. She also is a shapeshifter, one who can change appearance from animal to human. Her leading man is Renrengen, the wildman in the woods, an aspect of Ogun, the hunter-provider, the one who captures wild nature, tempers it, and turns it into tools for the use of humankind.

Their supporting casts consists of the two wives Oshun and Yemaya, the diviner, the villagers, the wind, and the trees. And, of course, we assume the invisible presence of Elegba, the Trickster who begins and ends all things. This story takes place in the crossroads between wild nature and material civilization. The word "Owo" is used to speak of the work of one's hands and the money earned from such work.

No drums are heard tonight, only the sound of the agogô bells, bells to soothe the king's sorrow. Tonight, the bell players will go from village to village, compound to compound, searching in the dark, searching for Orunsen.

"Orunsen, where'd She go? Orunsen, You be She?" But Orunsen is never found!

Orunsen, the deer woman, came to the edge of the bush one morning before the sun began to rise. She looked about Her cautiously and spoke to the trees, the wind, and the forest spirits, entreating them with "No one must ever know!"

Then She slipped out of Her deerskin, folded it carefully, and hung it over a low branch in a place of equal shadow and light. Reaching into the bundle She carried on Her back, She took out a cloth the colors of sunset. Orusen wrapped Her body and Her head. She tucked Her tail, covered Her hairy patches, and concealed Her dwarf horns. Then She counted Her pots, brooms, and bangles and set out for the marketplace like a natural woman.

Soon after, along came Renrengen, the king of the hunters, searching for bush cow for the pots of His wives.

And He beheld a magnificent thing shimmering on the branch of a tree. The king touched the skin, and softness caressed His fingers; He inhaled, and perfume danced in His nose. The skin was whole and complete, and nowhere was there a trace of blood or the mark of a knife upon it.

"What manner of creature is this?" He wondered to Himself. Intoxicated by curiosity, the king hid in the bush and awaited the creature's return. The hours of the day passed slowly by, and the king fell into an enchanted sleep. It seemed to Him that now the trees were singing, and He struggled against an urge to dance with the wind.

As the Sun began to set, Renrengen saw the light moving through the bush. In dazzling orange and purple, She stood there, Her skin a dusky copper tone. The king came out from His hiding place, beguiled—for, in all His life and in all the world, He had never seen a woman as lovely and as mysterious as She. And He entreated Her immediately to come and be His wife.

But the woman only reached for Her skin.

At first, He asked for Her hand. Softly.

And She asked for Her skin. Softly.

Then He insisted that She give Him Her hand, Her hand, Her hand.

Until She begged for Her skin, Her skin, Her skin.

Finally, stuffing Her skin into His sack, the king commanded that She come with Him and be His wife in Owo. Under duress, She agreed on the condition that He take great care of Her skin and one day return it to Her. She knew that, until that day, She would have to try to maintain this form so She could live among the humans.

The king led the deer woman through the bush to the town of Owo. That night They slept together in His hut, and Renrengen was satisfied as never before. Afterwards, Orunsen listened to the sound of leaves falling, birds singing, and humans moving about, weary from maintaining Her human form, yet too nervous to sleep.

The king's wives Oshun and Yemaya were up all night as well, watching and worrying, wondering, and waiting for Renrengen's return. When the sun rose, They went to the hut of the king, and there They found this mysterious woman.

Oshun snatched the covers from Them and bellowed, "Is this what You have brought for Our pot? Who is She?"

The king snapped to His feet and replied, "This is My new wife, Orunsen!"

The king's wives looked Him in the eye and reminded Him that although He was entitled to more than one wife, He was, by custom, obliged to provide for every wife He had, and because He'd failed to bring home any meat last night, He had get back into the bush and do His job.

Quickly, Renrengen gathered up His hunting gear and informed His wives that He would go into the bush again and that this time, when He returned, He would have enough meat for three pots. With that, He nodded to Orunsen and was off.

Now Orunsen was alone with His wives. Oshun and Yemaya walked in a circle around Her, looking Her up and down, shaking Their heads and clicking Their tongues. They questioned Her, and, as best She could, She replied.

"Who is Your mother?"

"Oh, You wouldn't know My mother!"

"Where is Your village?"

"My village? Uh, it's a long way away from here."

"When was Your wedding?"

"Sometime late last night?"

Finally, Oshun shouted angrily, "I am first wife, why was I not consulted?"

Orunsen knew that these women were well within their rights to be skeptical and that She was without Her skin. So She decided to be quiet. She picked up Her jug, placed it on Her head, and went down to the river to fetch water with the other women.

As the women walked down to the river, They sang, "Iyami ile odo. Iyami ile odo." ("My mother's house is in the water.")

When They reached the river, the other women dipped Their water pots, filled them, and played in the stream. Orunsen, who was tired from standing upright so long, knelt down on all fours. After filling Her belly with the sweet water, She fell asleep.

From downstream, Oshun and Yemaya watched Her, and They were aghast!

"Look!" said Oshun. "She laps Her water like a dog!"

"Yes," said Yemaya, "and She sleeps at the stream like an animal!"

The women drew closer to quietly examine the slumbering Orunsen. They moved the cloth on Her body and head, and there They found the semblance of horns and tail. Then They knew that there was a bush creature among Them!

So They ran back to the village, to the hut of the king, and tucked away in a corner They found it—They found Her skin! With great contempt They commenced to rip, rip, rip it to pieces.

Back at the river, Orunsen awoke to a great pain running up Her back. She tossed and rolled, writhing in misery and pain. "My skin!" She cried out, and She began galloping back to the village like an antelope.

When She reached the hut of the king, She found Her skin tattered and torn, battered and bruised, rolled in the dirt, and spat upon.

What was She to do? Surely the king would be condemned for bringing an animal to live in the house with Him! She could not stay in the village. But without Her skin, She could not live in the bush! She was caught between the worlds, belonging to neither and both.

Orunsen invoked the wisdom of the wind and, after doing so, decided to return to the bush to die. As she stumbled through the forest, the trees wailed a song: "Orunsen Owo. Iya Owo. Orunsen Owo. Iya Owo'runsen. . . ." ("Orunsen is the mother of Owo.")

When the king returned and found Orunsen gone, He fell into a deep depression. He wouldn't eat, He couldn't sleep, He refused to hold high counsel. Soon His enemies began to plot against Him. And worse, the people suffered. The rain would not fall, the crops did not grow, young women did not conceive, and those who were pregnant delivered dead babies!

Oshun, being the first wife and a wise woman, went to the Babalawo to divine on the meaning of this.

The diviner cast cowrie shells and palm nuts and declared, "Osa Ogunda." The interpretation was clear: "Homage must be paid to a creature, half woman, half deer. Then and only then will the town of Owo be restored!"

The women of the village gathered in the bush, bringing offerings of food and cloth, song and praise. Suddenly the forest was ablaze with the colors of sunset, orange and purple shimmering in a copper globe. Then a voice rang out like a bell: "When I was on Earth, the humans were cruel to Me. But now I have gone to live with Olorun in the sky. Erect a shrine to Me and respectfully bring offerings and prayers. So long as you do this, I will watch over your town. I will bring fertility, prosperity, and peace."

The people did as She said, and Owo flourished.

This is why every year, in the dry season, the drums are quiet, and the people go through the village and out into the bush, playing the agogô bell and calling, "Orunsen, where She go? Orunsen, You be She?"

Gail Williams, *Shango Oba Koso 2 BW*. 2022.

THE LEGEND OF OBAKOSO

This is a story of power and the abuse of power, of courage and foolhardiness, of betrayal and loyalty. Reprising the now familiar figures of Shango, Timi, and Gbonka, it bespeaks the Yoruba requirement for leadership and the remedy for political power out of balance. All power to the people!

When Shango was the king, the Oba of Old Oyo, He had two faithful soldiers, two brothers named Timi and Gbonka.

The three of them had fought many battles. Together they'd built a powerful cavalry, subdued the mighty army of Dahomey four times, and pushed back invaders who sold people as slaves. At last, a time for peace had come.

When Shango and His soldiers returned from battle, the people celebrated. They paid tribute in a great festival with food and gifts, music and dancing, and songs that praised the prowess of their army. The people placed a crown of beads upon Shango's head and declared Him the Alaafin, The Owner of the Royal Palace.

As the sun set on the festival, Timi and Gbonka laid down their weapons, ready to join the community in their days of peace.

Shango entered His palace and sat on His throne. He sank into the softness of a leopard skin cushion and rested

His arms on gigantic ram horns that adorned both sides of the chair. A large calabash filled with money cowries, a turtle shell rattle, and a double-headed ax lay at His feet. Proudly He sat there, day after day.

He sat there, and sat there, and sat there.

He could do that because He was the king, you know.

Meanwhile, Timi and Gbonka helped the people to restore the land, to build their homes, and to educate the children. The villagers rejoiced. Their voices rang throughout the royal compound. Shango heard them say:

> *Timi and Gbonka planted a field of yams yesterday.*
> *Timi and Gbonka built a new community house today.*
> *Timi and Gbonka will roast bushmeat for the feast*
> *tomorrow.*
>
> *Timi and Gbonka poured libations for the ancestors.*
> *Timi and Gbonka told stories to the children.*
> *Timi and Gbonka helped the elders to bed last night.*

But the people no longer spoke of His mighty deeds, *His* victory in war. Had He been forgotten? He thought that was not right because **He was the king, you know!**

A strange feeling seized Him. It hardened His jaw, soured His stomach, and set His eyes on fire.

This is called JEALOUSY.

The King shook His turtle shell rattle loudly. The sound summoned Timi to His side.

Timi bowed his head, lowered his eyes, and lifted his heels in deference. "Yes, Kabiyesi?"

Shango asked, "How are things in the village today?"

"Things are fine, Oba. Gbonka and I plowed the field at the year-round farm. Tomorrow the women will plant a crop of honey beans."

"Indeed," Shango replied. Then He added, "Timi, I want you to fight Gbonka in the public square tomorrow. For the entertainment of the people."

Timi chuckled and said, "But Kabiyesi, my brother and I have more work to do."

Timi's response irritated Shango. **Because He was the king, you know.**

"*Do it,*" Shango insisted, giving Timi a handful of cowries.

Timi placed the cowries in the bag that hung from his waist. "Yes, Kabiyesi," He said as he bowed and backed up through the open door.

The next day Timi gathered the people in the public square. The two brothers circled each other as if they were about to fight. But when Timi shook his medicine bag, Gbonka fell as if in sleep, and the cowries from the King spilled to the ground.

The people gratefully gathered the cowries and said to each other:

> *Those brothers are always playing around.*
> *Timi and Gbonka are so much fun.*
> *Timi and Gbonka had us laughing so much.*
> *Timi and Gbonka love to entertain the children.*
> *Timi and Gbonka know how to work and to play.*

Timi and Gbonka are both so handsome.
Timi and Gbonka are loved by all the girls.

This laughter from the square outraged Shango, sitting still on His throne, because the people still did not speak of Him. That was wrong. **Because He was the king, you know!**

So He shook His rattle to summon Gbonka to His side. Gbonka came quickly.

Shango lifted His chin and looked down on the man as He spoke. "Gbonka, everybody is laughing at you because Timi beat you in the public square yesterday."

Gbonka smiled and bowed his head as he answered. "Yes, Kabiyesi, it's true I fell asleep."

Shango snorted. "You must defend yourself next time."

Gbonka shrugged his shoulders. "But, Kabiyesi, what does it matter? Timi is my brother. We were just playing around."

"Do it!" Shango insisted, laying a string of magnificent beads around the man's neck.

The next day the two brothers met the people in the marketplace to perform the battle again. When Timi made to lunge at his brother, Gbonka played a rhythm on His drum—a rhythm so powerful that the string around His neck exploded and showered the people in beautiful beads.

The people gathered up those beads and danced out of the marketplace, raving about the performance saying:

"Those brothers are always playing around.
Timi and Gbonka played those drums.
Timi and Gbonka danced.
Timi and Gbonka let the children laugh.
Timi and Gbonka had such beautiful beads.
Timi and Gbonka made the young girls smile.
Timi and Gbonka! Those brothers are always playing
around."

From His throne, Shango heard them applauding! He was furious because the people still had not called His name. The insult felt like a punch in His gut. The pain of it consumed Him. How could this be?

He was the KING, you know!

Now He shook the rattle oh so loudly to summon Timi once more. Timi arrived and humbly saluted Shango, as was the custom.

Shango rose from His throne and circled Timi slowly. Abruptly He stepped to Timi and glared with burning eyes. "Timi, Gbonka has been talking bad about yo momma!" He bellowed.

Timi stood still and suppressed a smile. "But Kabiyesi, what does it matter? He's my brother. We have the same mother."

Shango reached for His double-headed axe, circled it above Timi's head, and commanded, "Hear Me clearly: you kill Gbonga, or I'll kill you!"

Timi backed out of the open door and ran to see his brother.

The two brothers sat on the mat to share bean cakes and chew kola nuts as they prayed over the matter. What had they had done to anger the Oba? They'd entertained the people. They'd done everything He asked. They remembered His courage and His strength and the battles they'd won under His direction. But now He wanted them to fight each other!

They agreed that even if they both fought Him, they couldn't win because Shango was the greatest warrior in all of Oyo.

And so they had to do what He asked because He was the king, you know.

The next day the people followed the brothers into the courtyard of the royal compound. This time they did not circle each other or laugh or jest in any way.

Instead, they bowed to each other.

When Timi brandished his cutlass, Gbonka offered Timi his throat. And Timi slew Gbonka. The people gasped, the children screamed, the young girls cried, and the elders spit.

Timi impaled His brother's head on the edge of the blade and processed slowly to Shango's palace.

Along his way, the people implored, "Timi, why have you done this terrible thing? How could you? *Gbonka was your brother!*"

Timi lowered his head as he dragged his feet in the dirt. "I didn't want to do it. Shango made me do it!"

The procession arrived at the palace, and Timi laid his brother's head at Shango's feet and asked, "Are you satisfied now, Kabiyesi?"

The people were angry.

"What kind of man is this Shango?" the women screamed as they shook their breasts.

A young man shouted, "You are not fit to rule!"

The Ogboni handed Him a covered calabash and walked away holding their heads.

Shango felt a knot in His stomach. His chin fell to His chest, and His eyelids would not lift themselves.

This is called Shame!

Shango accepted the gourd, anticipating the Council's judgment. Then the people threw stones and hurled fire at His palace.

While clutching the calabash, He ran into the Forest of Forever. Branches slapped His face and dirt clouded His eyes. His foot slipped, and He fell into a mound of fire ants.

Finally, He stopped at the foot of the majestic iroko tree, took a deep breath, and reviewed His life as the king. He remembered the many battles He'd fought, the soldiers He'd trained, and the women He'd loved in His lifetime. He remembered the loyalty of Timi and Gbonka and the praise they'd received from the people. It all seemed so unfair because **He was—**

He opened the covered calabash.

In it, He saw a cluster of parrot eggs and knew **He was the king no more.**

Shango cracked the eggs and closed the calabash. Then He grabbed a sturdy vine, wrapped it around His neck, and hung Himself so that His hunger for power would harm the people no more.

A messenger, a priest of Elegba, was summoned to enter the Forest of Forever and report his findings to everyone. Upon discovering Shango's body hanging from that tree, the messenger ran through the village announcing:

"Oba So, Oba So, the king is hung!
Oba So, Oba So, the king is hung!"

Shango's mother, Yemaya, went to the iroko tree. When She saw Her baby boy hanging there, She cried, "Oh, My poor boy! My only son is dead!" She wept Herself into an ocean of tears.

When His lover Oshun arrived, She hugged His body and cried: "My brave man. How could You leave Me like this?" She was so pained and embarrassed that She flowed downriver and out of town.

A great wind rustled through the trees, and the forest trembled as Oya fanned Her skirts. When She saw His body hanging there, She howled, "I will bury My champion's body no matter what!"

At the sound of Her voice, a hole in the earth opened. She placed the calabash of broken eggs in the earth and covered it with leaves. At that moment, a bolt of lightning struck the iroko tree, and suddenly Shango's body was gone!

The forest was still and silent for seemingly forever.

Then a thunderous voice spoke from the heavens, saying, "Oya, I am now in the heavens with Olorun. From this high place, I will watch over those who rule. Let My death serve as a reminder to them always that **the PEOPLE** *are* **the king, you know!"**

That evening, Elegba's messenger ran through the village, announcing:

"Oba Koso, Oba Koso, the king is not hung!
Oba Koso, Oba Koso, the king is not hung!"

THE CALABASH OF MISFORTUNE

During my performances of this story, I'd often ask, "Does anybody know what good fortune is?" And many times, people named things such as receiving a gift that you didn't expect, having things turn out better than you'd hoped, or having things always go your way.

Many years ago, I was preparing to tell this story at the Oakland Museum to an audience of parents and children. When I asked, "Does anybody know what bad fortune is?", a little boy raised his hand. He was so eager to answer that I called on him.

"Son, can you tell us what bad luck is?"

He stood up proudly and he said, "Bad luck is when you don't let people love you!"

The audience laughed nervously.

Right away I asked, "Where is this child's mother?" and when she raised her hand, I asked, "How old is he?"

She told me he was four years old.

It's often said that wisdom comes from the mouth of babes.

A long, long, long, long, long time ago, there was a couple, a woman and a man by the names of Tired and Disgusted.

No matter how hard they worked, they never had any money, and no matter how much they tried to, they never had a little baby of their own. So, they made themselves content with sitting outside their hut, eating raw turnips with oil and salt from a calabash of misfortune.

One day, Tired got so tired that she turned the calabash over and cried out to the sky, "I'm tired of eating from the calabash of misfortune!"

Just then, the Old Ones in the heavens heard her and answered her prayer. So They sent three blessings from heaven to Earth: Money, Child, and Patience.

The three blessings put on their backpacks, and they started the long journey down Crystal Mountain to go from heaven to Earth. But first, they came upon the river!

Money looked at Child and said, "Child, I'm an old man. You need to carry me across this river."

But Child disagreed. "Money, I'm just a little bitty fellow. You are tall and strong; you *have to* carry me."

"No, *you* have to carry *me*."

"No, *you* have to carry *me*."

Meanwhile, Patience had simply lifted her skirt and walked across the river. Still, Money and Child argued for quite some time.

Finally, Patience said, "I'll carry you both."

Again, she lifted her skirt and crossed the river. She put Money on one shoulder and Child on the other. Bearing the weight of them both, she stepped carefully on the slippery rocks that led to the riverbank.

When she got to the other side of the river, she put them both on their feet, and they continued the journey, Money and Child arguing every step of the way. Patience just took one step at a time, moving purposefully toward the village.

When they finally arrived at the hut of Tired and Disgusted, Patience explained to the couple that although the Old Ones had sent three blessings from heaven to Earth, they could only *keep* one!

Oh, my goodness, what should they do?

Tired and Disgusted discussed it and discussed it, but they could not come to an agreement.

So, Tired went to the women's society, and she told them about the choice they had to make.

The women said, "Girl, take the Money. You will need money to run your house and to feed your child. Take your money to Ejibomekun Market, and you'll never be hungry again."

Tired returned to the hut, but when she told Disgusted what the women said, he didn't agree.

So Tired and Disgusted discussed it and discussed it, but they could not come to an agreement.

Disgusted said, "Let me talk to the men's society," and off he went to meet with the boys.

The men said, "Man, take the Child. Because when your child has a child, through him, you'll live forever."

Excited, Disgusted said, "Yeah! I'd love to have a son!" After he passed out cigars, he headed for home.

But when He got home and told Tired what the men decided, she said, "Uh huh. But if there is no money to *feed* your child, your child won't live to *have* a child, child!"

Sadly, he knew she was right.

So Tired and Disgusted discussed it and discussed it, and finally they agreed that the best choice was to take Patience.

But when they told the men and women of their decision, the people sucked their teeth and said, "You fools, that's why you ain't got nothing now! Too much patience."

Even so, Tired and Disgusted told Patience to settle into their hut, for she was going to live with them for a long time.

Accepting their lot, Money and Child put on their backpacks and began the long walk to Crystal Mountain so they could return to heaven from Earth.

But then, of course, they came upon the river.

Child said, "I'm just a little bitty fellow, Money. Carry me."

Money complained, "I'm an old man, Child. Carry me."

"No, *you* carry *me!*"

"No, *you* carry *me!*"

As they argued, the river raged. Finally, they called out, "Patience, can you come get us please?"

From Tired and Disgusted's hut, she heard their cry. So, she got out of her bed and went down to the river. She put Money on one shoulder and Child on the other.

Just as she stepped into the river, the heavens opened!

Thunderous voices laughed. "Patience, We've been watching this whole thing from up here. Money and Child have behaved badly, so We're not sure We want them back up here. Would you like to keep them?"

"Oh yes, please, I'd love to keep them," Patience answered. "Thank You. I did not want to cross the river another time, to tell You the truth."

So Money and Child went to live with Patience in the hut of Tired and Disgusted, and they all lived happily ever after.

Children are cute, and Money is nice, but the person who keeps Patience gets everything by and by. Good luck!

Gail Williams and Luisah Teish, *Oshun, Shango & Obatala.*
2022.

PART III:
THE CASTING

THE MERMAID'S LOVER

One of the most alluring creatures in world mythology is the mermaid. The mermaid is usually depicted as a creature with a human face and upper body but with her bottom half covered in scales and supported by fins and webbed appendages.

All though mermen exist, most often they show up in mythology as secondary characters to the mermaids.

Because of popular media, most people have skewed vision of the mermaid. In 1989, Disney portrayed the mermaid as Ariel, the red-haired little white girl with the big eyes and the sweet voice. This mermaid, inspired by Hans Christian Andersen's story, falls in love with a human and suffers greatly to win his love. She is a victim of the patriarchal interpretation of myth, just like Obba.

But the image and the story of Disney fame do not match the ancient conception of the mermaid found in many cultures around the world. In world mythology, the mermaid is beautiful, seductive, secretive, and deceptive. She may live in the middle of the ocean and, like the sirens of Greek lore, drive men crazy with her singing as she destroys their boats. Or she may hang out between the rocks in brackish water, waiting for her next victim to arrive.

In West Africa, the mermaid Mami Wata is a goddess who brings dreams, performs healings, and possesses devotees in ceremonies. Elusu, the *mae d'agua* (mermaid) in our story, was transported from West Africa to Brazil. Her skin is chalk white because devotees of Mami Wata cover their bodies in white chalk when they perform rituals at the ocean under the blazing sun—also because Elusu lives deep in the ocean, where the sun does not shine.

In our story, it's the young man who falls in love with the mermaid.

You've seen him: the boy who sits on a rock at the edge of the ocean, gazing at the horizon. You've seen him sitting there.

One morning at just about sunrise, Inle was sitting there on that rock at the edge of the ocean. As he looked out, he saw a glimmer of sunlight reflecting on the water. And it moved closer and closer and closer. When the light stopped just beneath the rock where he sat, he looked down, and he saw Her: Elusu, the mermaid.

When he reached for Her, She lifted one fin-finger and said, "Ah, ah, ah. Not for you to love Me, boy."

Struck with amazement, he left the rock and went running, running home to talk to his brother. "Oh, brother. Brother, I've seen Her! I've seen Elusu, the mermaid."

His brother said, "Boy, you've been sitting out on that rock again? You need to come home and play ball with me and the other fellas."

So, Inle picked up the ball, bounced it a few times, and went on about his business.

But the next day found him sitting on that rock at the edge of the ocean. You've seen him sitting there, many times. He looked at the waves in the light of the sun at high noon. Again, he saw a beautiful blue glimmer moving toward him. Again, She came near the rock, and he looked into the pearly eyes of Elusu, the mermaid.

He reached for Her, and She shook Her fin-finger. "No, no, no, it's not for you to love Me, boy."

Inle was enchanted with the beauty of the mermaid. She had chalk white skin, seaweed green hair, pearly blue eyes, and a fish scale body. But again, She pulled away from him, and he ran home.

He reported to his father, "Father, I've seen Her! Elusu, the beautiful, beautiful mermaid."

And his father said, "Boy, you better leave that mermaid alone. Better men than you have been lost at sea, messing with Her. Now go to your room; go do something."

Inle tried to listen; he really tried, but the next day found him, at sunset, sitting on that rock, watching for that wave, smelling the salt spray of the sea.

And as She drew closer, he reached down to touch Her. She shook the fin-finger and said, "Uh, uh, uh, it's not for you to love Me, boy."

As blood rushed through his body, he yearned to touch this mermaid. She withdrew into the water, and he ran home to his mother. He found her on her knees, scrubbing the floor with work-worn hands.

"Mama, Mama," he said, "I've found my wife."

And his mother assumed, "You want to marry Fanta, the girl next door? Good, son. That's good, son!"

And he said, "Oh, no, Mama."

"Not Fanta? Then who?"

He said, "Mama, *I love Her.*"

"Who?" his mother asked. "You love who?"

He replied, "Elusu, the mermaid."

When he said Her name, his mother's face turned an ashy gray. She stopped her work, dropped her head, and wrung her hands nervously. "Son, please, promise me you won't go near that treacherous mermaid. Please, son, promise me you'll stay away from Her. Promise! Promise, do you promise?"

Inle made that promise to his mother.

But as much as he tried, in the middle of the night, he found himself sneaking out to go sit on the edge of that rock. And in the darkness under the light of a full moon, She swam up to the rock's edge and lingered near him. She studied him closely with her pearly eyes; She showed him Her seaweed hair, Her firm breasts and long arms, Her blue and purple scales.

And this time, She touched his face with Her tail.

Her touch was intoxicating. He leaned over the edge of the rock, longing to touch just one fin.

Just then, Elusu pulled him down into the water.

As She pulled him deeper into the water, she chanted,

"Ooo me tu tu,
ooo na tu tu.
Ooo me tu tu,
ooo na tu tu.
Ooo me tu tu,
ooo na tu tu. . . ."

commanding the path to the deep to open for Her.

He could feel himself moving through the waves, moving through the seaweed, moving past the corals, moving,

moving. He saw so many fish—until finally, he and the mermaid rested on the bottom of the ocean.

Inle looked around him and saw a panorama of a magnificent scene. An entire underworld. He saw an underworld forest. He saw an underworld zoo! He saw an underworld solar system, and he knew that he was in another world.

In the distance, there was a castle. And Elusu led him there, where they lived for quite some time.

On the surface of the water, Inle's family, neighbors, and friends formed a group. They searched for him. They searched for him in the morning but saw no sign of him. They looked around the rocks at high noon—no sign of him. They searched as the sun was setting. They looked for him every night for seven nights. But they never did see a trace of him. In some parts of West Africa, when someone disappears and is not found for seven nights, the people say, "Matduma got them." Inle's community agreed that "the dark mystery" must have swallowed him.

But way down beneath the water, inside the castle of Olokun, Inle was as happy as he could be. His beautiful, beautiful mermaid pinned Her hair in a bun, donned an apron, and took off Her jewels. And down there, they lived happily as She cooked for him. And She cleaned for him. And She took care of him, always wiping Her hands on that heavy, heavy apron She wore.

Inle, meanwhile, never bothered to do anything. He didn't even notice anything except that he was being taken care of, and he especially paid no attention to the weight of the apron that Elusu wore.

Every night, after working so hard for him, She would retire to a room in the back of the castle and slam the door. When they first got together, Inle said it was all right for Her to have a private room. He thought to himself, *You know, most women like to have their own space, and after all, you know, She cooks, and She cleans, and She takes care of me. So what if She has a secret chamber that She retires to every night?*

So he promised that he'd never enter it, and for a time he was very happy. But, after many moons, he longed to know what was behind that door.

So, he asked Her, "Why can't I go into Your inner chamber?"

And She said, "Because it's Mine."

"But why can't *I* go into Your inner chamber?"

And She said, "Because every woman has secrets."

And then he did what many men seem to feel they must do: he challenged Her with, "*But* if You love me . . . *If* You love me . . . If You *love me*, You will let me see Your inner most secrets!"

(*Hm.*)

Elusu surrendered to his plea. "All right," She said, wiping Her hands on Her apron. "I do love you. So I'll let you into My secret chamber. But you must promise to never tell anyone what you see there."

He touched his heart and swore on all that was wet that he would never, ever give away Her secret. And that promise made him remember another one he'd once made, to somebody else—but that left his mind as Elusu, the beautiful, beautiful mermaid, opened the door to Her inner chamber.

A bright light, such as he had never seen, softer than the moon yet brighter than the sun, almost blinded him. Inle stepped into the room, and his eyes slowly adjusted to the light. The floor was covered in beautiful shells. The ceiling was crystal, and the walls were decorated with the most amazing colors of all the fish in the sea. As he looked around, he saw pirates' chests full of the finest jewels and gold doubloons. He saw ancient, precious artifacts—every treasure that had ever been lost at sea lying about casually. He walked around, looking at the riches. He dipped his hands in the treasure chests, and pearls slipped through his fingers.

He thought about his life above the water and all the things he could buy with all this wealth. He saw his mother's hands softly manicured and adorned in this fine jewelry.

He became so absorbed in thought that he uttered, "Wait until I tell Mother!"

But the second he said, "Mother," Elusu grabbed his tongue. She put Her hand in Her apron pocket, and out came Her machete. *Whack!*

She cut off Inle's tongue, and She ate it!

Blood ran from his mouth as he screamed in pain. He broke through the door and ran out of the castle. He ran out onto the sandscape and began to swim up, up, up, up.

He could feel, he could feel, he could feel himself changing—but he didn't know the magic invocation. What was it that She'd chanted when She brought him down?

"*Ooo mi tu tu*, something.
Ooo mi tu tu, somewhere.

Ooo mi tu tu, somehow.
Ooo mi tu tu, someone.
Ooo mi tutu, O me . . ."

But he just couldn't remember the chant.

And as he swam and swam and swam toward the surface, Inle realized his body was different. As he swam and swam and swam, he realized that his face was different. Still, he swam, and he swam, and he swam, and finally he broke the surface of the water and jumped up onto the rock.

Then he just sat there.

Because that's all he could do.

Now, I know you've seen him, the mermaid's lover, sitting on that rock, trying to tell someone what happened to him. You've seen his shining black skin. His big, luminous eyes. But all he can do, sitting there, is flap his fins and go, "*Ooh ohh! Ooh ohh! Oooh ohh!*"

That's him, the mermaid's lover. You've seen him, I know you have: the mermaid's lover, a seal, sitting on the rock at the edge of the sea.

Carla Johnson and Nedra Williams, *Olokun*. 1992.

OLOKUN'S CHALLENGE

The Blessed Binary

"God is No *Thing*, incomprehensible, and beyond
direct human contact. Earth, air, fire, and water in
all their myriad forms are only reflections of God
the creator. *Discussions on the gender of God are ab-
surd, and traditionally Africans do* not *attempt to
make images of the Infinite One.* Whatever we say
about God is limited by our *perception* of God; but
God is not limited."
—*Jambalaya*: *The Natural Woman's Book of Personal
Charms and Practical Rituals*

The sacred stories of the Edo people of Benin depict Olokun
as the most important deity. In the Edo view, Olokun is the
owner of all the earth's waters, and He has dominion over
all other water spirits. They state that all the waters of the
earth came from and return to Olokun. Olokun owned the
planet we now call Earth before Obatala placed the continents on His surface.

In Benin, Olokun is clearly envisioned as a male deity. His icon depicts the mudfish king, a man with a split
fish tail. He is rich, powerful, and highly praised. Devotion
to Olokun assures good health, wealth, prestige, and comfort. The Edo people have many stories about Olokun, and

His wife Ora is acknowledged as an integral part of His power. Conversely, in Yorubaland, Olokun is thought of as female and is sometimes called Yemidirigbe (Epega). She lives in the deep dark ocean and is envisioned as a beautiful, black-skinned mermaid who is both powerful and terrible. During the Middle Passage, Yemaya, the mother of the Ogun River in Nigeria, also came to be associated with the unfathomable expanse and depth of the ocean.

The Middle Passage was a horrendous journey. Human beings were packed like sardines in the bottom of the slave ships. They were raped and beaten and thrown overboard to lighten the load of dead bodies. Sometimes pregnant women and those who'd recently given birth preferred to jump into the ocean rather than become slaves in a foreign land. They surrendered to the loving embrace of the Great Mother Water.

For half a century, people in the diaspora debated the true nature of Olokun. It was even sometimes thought that, as the power at the bottom of the ocean, He was too great to speak of. After much cultural exchange, especially with Cuba, the deity's identity is resolved in Yemaya-Olokun. Yemaya-Olokun is androgynous[48] and gynandrous,[49] encompassing the blessed binary. I am grateful to my temple sister Nedra Williams, an Olokun priestess, for the many stories she has shared with me.

The classic tale of "Olokun's Challenge" predicts an endless power struggle between the sky and the ocean. This rendering of the tale proposes another possibility.

---

48   As the primarily male sky (via the sun) holds a female energy (the moon) within it.

49   As the primarily female earth (via the water) holds a male energy (the fire) within it.

Between the Sky and the Deep Blue Sea

In the beginning, all was covered in water, and Olokun, the lord of the deep, ruled the planet with His court of sea creatures. He rode the currents of the deep on the back of His turtle and entertained Himself by dancing with the jellyfish while the octopus vacuumed the floor of the sea.

Then Obatala, the King of the White Cloth, the lord of the clouds, descended on a golden chain, a beam of radiant sunlight, carrying a sack of cosmic dust and a five-toed guinea hen. Obatala dropped the sack of sand and released the hen, who scratched the continents into place. Then He returned to His place among the clouds. The sun shone brightly on the dark waters, and life on land began. A single cell divided into two and gave birth to seaweed, hydra, and fish.

Millions of Earth years passed, and evolution progressed. Soon the crab crawled out of the water, and human beings walked on the surface of the earth.

Olokun began to feel the weight of the earth. The rumblings from above intruded on the silence of the deep, and worst of all, some of His beautiful creatures began to disappear. Were the humans fishing?

He decided to defend His kingdom.

Olokun blew His conch shell, and His voice echoed across the water as the white caps rolled from sea to shore:

"Hear Me, all who live above. I, the tireless support of the sea, have grown weary of the weight of the earth. Before Asupa, the moon, rises tonight, I will change the tides of the ocean. I'll drag the moon across the sky, and I will send a tidal wave to devastate the land and every creature upon it. I'll wash it all away."

The roar of the conch and Olokun's threat traveled on the wings of the wind and reached the goddess Oya. She flew high above the mountains, being careful not to disturb Aganyu the volcano, and finally, resting on a rainbow, She whispered to Obatala, gently waking up the old man.

The wind blew softly between Her lips as She spoke: "Ibase,[50] Baba mi, I come to bring you the word."

Obatala, who had long ago tired of the noise and movement of commonplace existence, barely stirred from His sleep.

"The lord of the deep has threatened the earth with a tidal wave!" Oya continued. "But such a thing cannot be accomplished without my help, and I will not move without your blessing. Am I to cause an earthquake in the sea? Am I to send a wind to push the waves? Is this your wish, Baba?"

"No, Oya," Obatala mumbled in response. "Do not raise the wind nor disturb my sleep over such matters. I have watched the shifting of the sands, the drifting of the continents. I have seen the lava flow into the ocean where islands sprang up and mountains crumbled. It all changes in time, Oya."

---

50   Respect to the power of the spirit.

Oya danced in relief, the rustling of Her skirt painting a rainbow in the sky. She asked, "Very well, Baba, then what shall we do? How shall we respond?"

Obatala smiled as He looked at the rainbow and understood what He should do. "Oya, take Olokun's message to Agemo the Chameleon and tell Him to handle it for Me." Then Obatala laughed and fell back asleep smiling.

Oya wrapped Herself in Her rainbow shawl and took off for the Forest of Forever at the edge of the sea. There She found Agemo, who was very busy feasting on flies.

He stopped His meal to greet Her. "Good rising," He said. "How shall I earn the pleasure of your company?" Agemo rolled His eyes around, looking at the many colors in Her skirt.

He reached out, hoping to touch Her garment, but Oya swirled in place, and this forced Him to take a step back.

"I've come to you on behalf of Obatala," She reported.

"Oh, then it must be important," He said as He wrapped the flies in a leaf and tucked it away. "What does Baba wish of Me?"

She told Agemo about Olokun's threat to send a tidal wave to destroy everything on Earth.

As Agemo listened, His eyes rolled around and around. He extended His tongue and then snapped it back into His head. "Relax, Oya, be at ease. I know what I must do." And with that, He moved slowly to a low hanging branch that extended out over the ocean. There He made a croaking sound just loud enough to aggravate Olokun.

The ocean roared, and the white caps rolled across the surface of the water. Olokun parted the waves and rushing water washed the forest floor. "Who dares disturb my peace?" He demanded.

"I do, on behalf of Obatala," Agemo hissed. "I've come to meet Your challenge, Your threat to destroy the earth."

Olokun stepped on to land, luminous. His cape of blue-green seaweed sparkled. Its glowing light stretched across the sand for miles.[51]

He lifted His face to the heavens and bellowed, "Hear Me and see Me, Obatala. I come dressed in the power of plankton, the most important source of food in the sea. Perhaps You think that it is merely sea dust floating mercilessly in the tide. Not so. Oh, no. From the tiniest algae to the mightiest kelp forests, my luminous greens make their own living tissue from Your sun's energy. My turf produces half the oxygen in Your atmosphere. Still, Your ignorant humans intrude on My domain.

"Do You know how powerful I am?"

The sky did not respond.

Instead, Chameleon leapt from His branch on the tree and landed on Olokun, immediately matching Him in color and texture.

Agemo chuckled. "Olokun, Olokun. I see your fine green cape. Have You seen the many shades of green in the Forest of Forever where medicine grows, and each leaf is unique? It's iridescent. Ha ha ha. You ain't seen nothing yet."

Surprised by Chameleon's ability to match Him, Olokun stood silent. But only for a moment.

He inhaled the scent of the forest then dove into the Ocean, deliberately splashing water in Agemo's eyes. The surface of the water was still for what seemed like a long

---

51   Some varieties of plankton are bioluminescent.

time. Then suddenly Olokun emerged, and this time He was adorned in jewels. A thousand necklaces of deep red coral, silvery pearls, speckled shells, and sea glass shone in the sunlight.

Again, He addressed the Chameleon, who had returned to his usual green color. "Now, Chameleon, behold my coral. My reefs are rich and beautiful, more beautiful than any habitat on Earth."

Chameleon was careful not touch the beautiful flowers in the forest. He meandered past the pink bromeliads, stepped around the bright orange orchids, and completely avoided the red and yellow monkey brush vine.[52] He assessed the colors of His environment and then challenged the mudfish king.

"Olokun, Olokun, I see Your coral beads. Do You see the beautiful flowers? Can You smell their marvelous scent? Your coral beads are the bones of abandoned houses. These flowers renew themselves every spring."

After that careful walk, Agemo landed deliberately on the beads adorning Olokun's neck. And His entire body shed its green, reflecting instead the sea god's jewels.

With half of His split tail, Olokun slapped the Chameleon off His neck, and He crushed the monkey brush vine with the other half.

Seven times Olokun rose to the challenge, and seven times Chameleon matched His wealth and beauty with the colors of the land. The seventh time that Olokun returned to His domain, He lingered there a while. Then He sur-

---

52   A bright red and yellow flowering vine that grows in the rainforests. It is a resting place for certain small animals and a natural food source for tropical birds.

faced wearing a robe of blinding blue. It was as blue as the surface of the water, as blue as the sky above. Multicolored fish swam in the folds of His garment.

The Chameleon stepped back, remaining His own true color. Then He spoke to Olokun sympathetically: "Oh, king of the deep, no one doubts Your dominion over the sea, but You must understand that Your brilliant blue is only a reflection of Obatala's sky, and the fish are merely children of the rainbow who have fallen into the sea."

Exhausted now, Olokun considered that if Obatala's mere messenger could match Him in every way, then Obatala Himself must be an incredible power. At last, Olokun conceded and receded to the depths of the sea.

And the land was saved.

Well . . . at least that's the way the children of *Obatala* tell the story.

But one cannot be so sure—because the riches of the ocean *are* as vast as those of the land, and the statue of Olokun, the mudfish king of Benin, is often seen standing tall, proud, and holding a chameleon in each hand.

And what about the mermaid who, in the midst of all the praises of Obatala and of Olokun, surfed in on a wave and arrived on the shore just beneath the branch where Agemo sat?

The Chameleon rolled His eyes in wonder when he saw the mermaid sitting there on the shore. When She looked up at Agemo, the light from Her eyes was almost blinding. Her luminous black skin shone against the yellow sand,

and Her green seaweed hair was adorned with starfish and sea urchins. Her long, angular breasts stood up on their own, and a belt of sea snakes emerged from Her navel and cinched Her waist. Her bottom half, voluptuous, with fully rounded hips, was covered in a skin of scales that ran the length of those would-be legs, which met in a tail with seven layers of fins.

When She opened Her mouth, a spray of salty mist cleansed the atmosphere and sank into the sand around Her. "Hold it. Stop." She extended Her arms and silver bracelets rattled.

"That's the way the boys tell that story. They flash tongues and flip tails, showing off Their powers as They compete for possession of the earth. That's the reason We're in so much trouble already. Be quiet and listen, there's still another story to be told."

As Chameleon backed up a few steps on His branch, the monkey brush vine was hanging low. Olokun returned to the surface, and Obatala Himself woke up to listen. All the world was quiet as the mermaid sang Her siren song:

> *"They may kick and scream and cry*
> *Because those two maintain the lie*
> *That one is better than the other.*
> *In truth, all life comes from me . . .*
> *The mother."*

"Let me introduce myself," She continued, "though some of You already know Me very well." She cast a glance at Olokun. "I am Yemideregbe, the goddess of the sea. Look carefully so You can see the beauty, the power, the wealth that is Me. While you fellas argue over who is king, I here-by declare myself the queen of mystery. While Chameleon's ability to change colors is impressive, it is only a reflection of sunlight on His skin."

Chameleon lowered His head and said, "It's true, it's true. But what about You, queen mother? What is your magic? Where does your mystery lie?"

The mermaid stroked Her breasts and smiled. "I'm so glad You asked, My little lizard. The truth is, My waters are full of creatures who change in order to survive. Some are protogynous, born female then changing to male: the par-rotfish, the angelfish, and the damselfish, for example. Hm . . . is that why a woman in trouble is called a damsel in dis-tress? Ha ha, just kidding." She laughed, gently twisting Her hair. "Some of My creatures are protandrous, born male and changing to female, like anemonefish, snapper, and bass. It's quite a feat, don't You think?" She batted Her eyes at Olokun.

"Some others are simultaneous hermaphrodites, born both male and female at the same time. This happens a lot in the coral reefs. They make sure not to release their egg and sperm at the same time—to prevent self-fertilizing. Ya gotta keep a fork or two in the family tree, You know."

She winked at Olokun, and He lowered His eyes.

"But others, like the red and white starfish,[53] just break off an arm or a leg, go off, and grow into somebody else when they need to."

Now She raised Her head and addressed Obatala. "That's amazing. Don't You think so? Is there anything in Your creation that You'd like to change? Think about it, Obatala. You drank palm wine as You created humans."

---

53   Linckia multifora.

Obatala looked down and shook His head in regret.

Now, in the first iteration of the story, recall we were told that the lord of the deep was angry because of the weight of the human world on the seas. Ah, but now there is a deeper secret. The truth is whispered: *It was over an affair!*

When Olokun was asleep in the deep, his wife the sea goddess was penetrated by the luminous light of the sky. It was Her little tryst with Obatala that gave birth to the earth, that gave the earth all Her plants and Her animals, and that created a place for the humans.

So, you see, when Their daughter Earth was at stake, even the old man, Obatala, the King of the White Cloth, had to do something to save His daughter.

"Humans *are* my creations," Obatala admitted, a little wearily. "And the earth is My daughter!"

"No," Olokun growled, "She's Mine."

Now They began to confront each other directly. The Chameleon got out of Their way.

Olokun roared, "If I can't have Her, no one will. I'd sooner destroy everything."

Obatala countered, "We've already proven that I am greater than You!"

They raged at each other for a century or two. Finally, Their argument was interrupted by the sound of the mermaid's laughter.

"Olokun, Obatala. Obatala, Olokun. I'm not worried about either of You, really. You know what they say, 'momma's baby, daddy's maybe.' No doubt Earth is *My daughter*. The humans are the ones who get on My nerves."

Everyone was silent.

"Humans worry me," She went on. "I've cried over them for centuries. I've cried because of their wanton ways." Yemideregbe slumped and salty tears rolled down Her breasts. "I witnessed the African slave holocaust. Millions of people were packed into ships' bottom decks and carried across the Atlantic to be sold as slaves. And when the 'cargo' became too heavy, cried too loud, or ate too much, they were thrown overboard. Men, women, children, and babies. They cast living children into my waters. And I've washed their bones clean and held them to My breasts." The queen mother sobbed bitterly.

Oya, who'd held Herself back this entire time, flew forward to assist Her sister. She placed one of Her many arms around Yemi and wiped those tears with Her rainbow skirt.

"Oh yes, I was there," said Oya. "Foul winds blew around those ships. I counted the dead 9 x 9 x 9 x 9 x 9 x 9 x 9 x 9 x 9 to the 9th power dead. And still their bones rattle under the sea."

Yemi caught Her breath. "The humans. I've watched them sail across my waters escaping persecution, hunting for treasure, and displaying the booty of war and greed. I've watched them fuss, and fight, and kill."

"Indeed, My sister," Oya said. "The foul winds blow, pushing barges of plastic and garbage. Oil and blood, blood and oil, bombs and bullets, radioactive waste . . ."

Before Oya could take another breath, Yemi interrupted: "Too long I've tolerated the disrespect. Sonar on submarines disturbing My sleep. Oil spills and whale kills polluting My skin. Olokun, You claimed some of these same concerns, but out of competition and pride, never sorrow. Oh yes, I've cried, not only for Myself, but also for My many creatures. The dolphin, the sharks, and the whales. The humans have hunted them to extinction. How dare they kill My children!"

Moved deeply by Her sister's plight, Oya spoke. "They were here long before the humans, and they could be here long after the humans are gone. Just say the word, My sister, and I will raise the wind. I'll shake the mountain and let the volcano erupt. And You could stop the waves of the ocean."

The Chameleon dared to speak. "Great mothers, wait, wait! Please give them a chance to change. Give the humans a chance to do better."

Oya and Yemi looked at each other, then at Obatala and Olokun. The women spoke in unison.

"We will not damage the earth." They turned to Obatala and Olokun. "And neither will You." They turned to the Chameleon and said, "Take this message to the humans now: you have one more chance to change—but only one more."

The gods of the sky and of the deep nodded Their agreement. Obatala returned to His bed of luminous clouds. Olokun went down to His castle below. Yemi and Oya danced on the surface of the water.

And the Chameleon set off on His journey to tell the world, "One more chance. One more chance . . ."

And His body reflected all the colors of the rainbow.

PEACE NANA

We are blessed to live together on this beautiful planet, at this most important time. As we dance to the rhythm of life, our blended energies create the music of the spheres. Imagine now the joy of the creatrix, our mother, as She shaped us, colored us, named us, and provided the inspiration in us to create a variety of cultures.

At this time when our existence is threatened by our own behavior, a little humility, a willingness to be guided by Her, can still the hand of extinction. We can survive.

Even more, let us each examine the gifts of our respective cultures, the wisdom acquired from our experiences, the innovations fermenting in our minds, and the resilience of our spirits. Then, under Her guidance, let us join hands around the globe so that we may thrive.

This poem is a prayer to our great mother, requesting radical transformation.

Iba'che[54] NaNa, Womb of Creation,
She Who Gave Birth to All Things.
From Your dark depths, the first spark came into Being.

---

54   Respect to the power of the Spirit.

Your luminous Egg exploded in the midst of eternal night.
Its joyous dance formed the great lights.

You Who Gave Us Sun and Moon, Earth and Sky, Body
   and Spirit,
awaken from Your sleep, Deep Night.
Lift Your eyelids and see our plight.
The children of Earth are in need of Your guidance.
They await the feel of Your hand.
They roll their eyes in great suspicion.
In anger and fear they strike out.
Their hearts are hard; their hands are trembling.
Amidst the rubble of war, they cry out.

Hear me, Great Mother, hear your daughter:
Open Your starlight thighs. Draw us back in through Your
   vulva.
Mold our heads;
pat our behinds.
Change us, every cell and spirit, till Peace possess our minds.
Blow Your perfumed breath upon us;
wash us in the deep blue sea.
Suckle us on milk and honey;
oil us with the balm of love.

Return us then to this green garden,
oh Beautiful, Generous Mother,
but this time
give us the wisdom to see Your reflection
in one another.

THE WISHING STAR

This is another of my favorite stories. I've performed it at churches, community centers, and elementary schools around the world. Because I tell the story from a child's point of view, all the children love it, remember it, and sometimes they repeat the lines as I tell the story.

There is a popular belief in African diasporic culture that requests made to the "ancestors in heaven" are granted. So, we tell our children to "wish upon a star."

In this telling, I substitute the Orishas for the Haitian deities because They are more popular. In my telling, the Haitian Legba (an old man) becomes Elegba, the curious child. Haitian Agwe, the old man of the sea, is replaced by Yemaya, the nurturing mother. The coarse fellow Ogun is depicted as Yemaya's husband and Elegba's father. Here, Shango is Elegba's flirtatious uncle.

And of course, Nana Buluku is the wise grandmother of them all.

It was still dark morning, and my friend Elegba was out taking His morning walk. He was going where He wanted to go, to do what He wanted to do, to whomever He wanted to do it to. And as He walked along in the dark morning, there was a distant light that moved closer and closer and closer until—whoa! It fell to Earth in front of Him!

He looked down at it and said, "What's that thing? And what am I gonna do with it?" He tried to touch it, but it was hot. So, He went and called His mama. "Yemaya!"

Well, Yemaya was in the kitchen cooking Her breakfast, and She really didn't want to be bothered, but since He called Her, She wiped Her hands on Her apron and went over to Him.

When She saw a piece of light, She said, "Honey, what's that thing? And what are we gonna do with it?"

And Elegba said, "I don't know, Mama. I was just walking along, minding My own business when—whoa! That thing came flying out of the sky."

And Yemaya looked at it and said, "Well, it certainly is hot." So She fanned Her skirt around it and cooled it off with some ocean water. But She still didn't know what it was or what She was going to do with it.

She decided to call Her husband. "Ogun, honey, can You come look at this thing?"

Well Ogun was in the backyard, working on His car. And He really didn't want to be bothered.

But since She called Him, He came to where His wife and son were standing, and He said, "Woman, what's that thing? And what are You gonna do with it?"

And Yemaya said, "I don't know, honey, but it was awfully hot, and I cooled it off."

Elegba said, "I was just walking along minding My own business, Daddy, when—woah! That thing came flying out of the sky!"

Ogun looked at it, and He took a heavy, heavy chain, and He wrapped it around that thing and locked that thing up.

Well, He'd locked it up, but He still didn't know what it was or what He was going to do with it. At that point Ogun decided to call His brother: "Hey, Shango, man, come take a look at this thing!"

Well, Shango was standing on the corner, talking to His girlfriend. And when They called Him, He kissed Her twice, strutted toward Them, and said, "Say, brother. What's that thing? And what are We gonna do with it?"

Ogun said, "I don't know, man, but I locked it up."

Yemaya said, "It was awfully hot, and I cooled it off."

And Elegba said, "I was just walking along, minding My own business, Uncle, when—whoa! That thing came flying out of the sky."

Shango said, "Oh yeah? Well, I'll tell you what I'm gonna do with it." And He used Ogun's chains to tie that thing to one of His lightning bolts.

All the Orishas ran to follow the lightning bolt. It landed in front of Nana Buluku's house.

Nana had been asleep for thousands of years. But when that thing fell, She woke up and found all these Orishas standing around Her.

"Hmm?"

The other Orishas explained that this thing had fallen from the sky.

And can you guess what She said as She looked at it?

"Whose thing is this?"

Well, that's when the Orishas began talking all at once.

Shango said, "Well, it's Mine because I brought it here."

Ogun said, "Oh, no, I'm the one who chained it up."

Yemoja said, "It was awfully hot, and I cooled it off."

And Elegba said, "I was just walking along, minding My own business, Grandmother, when—whoa! That thing came flying out of the sky."

And They began to argue over whose thing it was.

Nana said, "Mhmm. Y'all discuss it, and let Me know."

Then She slept for a million years. And do you know that when She woke up, They were *still* arguing over that thing?

At that point, Nana said, "Well, since You don't know what it is, and You don't know whose it is, and You don't know what You're going to do with it, I'm going to do this—"

And She picked it up and hurled it into the sky.

And it's been there ever since.

Now, I wanna ask you: how many times have you looked at the sky at night? Have you seen that great, big ball of light that's in the sky sometimes at night?

What's that thing? *The moon.*

Now, sometimes the moon has had a lot of good stuff to eat, and Her belly sticks out. That's what we call a full moon.

And sometimes, the moon gets skinny, and She look like a crooked banana. That's what we call a crescent moon.

And sometimes, if you look up into the sky, you'll see a little bitty star hanging out around the moon's belly button. That's called a star and crescent.

And that is the Wishing Star.

So the next time you look up in the sky, and you see that star hanging out around the moon's belly button, I want you to point at the moon and make a wish, very, very carefully. After you make your wish, you point at the moon, and you say, "That's what it is; that's what They did with it."

And then you point to your heart, and you say, "And it's mine"—because that's how we first got the Wishing Star.

The people of old Dahomey in West Africa say, *As long as you keep a light in your heart, your wishes will always come true.*

So, that's what that thing is.

Nedra Williams, *Irosun Meji*. 2022.

APPENDICES

WISDOM WAYS

The wisdom ways are an invitation to dip your hand into the calabash and pick up some cowries. This section contains questions to inspire your reflections on the meaning of the stories. There are recommendations for charms to ignite your creativity, and there are guidelines for a variety of rituals. Elaborations on some of them can be found in *Jambalaya: The Natural Woman's Book of Personal Charms and Practical Rituals*. All of the offerings in the wisdom ways are designed to provide a new perspective, to help you digest ancient wisdom, and to integrate that wisdom into the practices of your daily life.

They are beautiful shells. Consult them, exchange them, and wear them freely.

Part I

The Creation

• Find a creation story from your culture and one from another culture. Compare the elements of the two. What is similar? What is different? Who are the characters in the tale, and what work do they perform?

• Combine elements from the two myths and write your own creation story. How might this new story guide your behavior?

The Coming of the Orishas

• Research the pantheon of deities from three different cultures. How are they similar? How are they different?

Oshun Learns the Art of Divining

• Do you feel that the Trickster works for you and your goals (good luck) or against you (bad luck) most of the time?

• Elegba comes along and performs the "trick" that gives Oshun the opportunity to turn the tide. Can you recount a time when an "accidental occurrence" helped you to shift the balance of power in a situation? What was the trick, and how did you use the advantage it provided?

• Obatala asks, "What is the King of the White Cloth without His white cloth?" In your opinion, what is the meaning of that outcry?

• Oshun "exchanged favors" with Elegba to acquire the white cloth. What price did She pay? What are you willing to do to acquire knowledge? Make an offering to Oshun in gratitude for making knowledge accessible to the multitudes.

The Oshun Honey Rinse

Oshun enchants both Elegba and Obatala with the power awakened in Her after the bath. When you are embarking on a journey through mystery, you can increase your chances of success by using the Oshun honey rinse.

You will need:

> • One gallon of river water (acquired by leaving an offering of five oranges at the river) or bottled spring water

> • An enchanting scent or perfume (such as jasmine, geranium, or plumeria oil)

> • One jar of wildflower honey (organic)

> • A large bowl or bucket

> • A big white towel

- Three yards of yellow silk fabric or a skirt with five yellow silk scarves fastened to the waist

- An anklet of bells for your left foot

Directions:

- Take a bath as you normally would with the intention of washing away any feeling of lack, inability, or shortcoming. Focus especially on releasing the negative effects of other people's discouragement about your abilities, their judgments of you. Take at least fifteen minutes to let the memories and feeling come to the surface. Then drain the water out of the tub (or rinse yourself in the shower).

- Put the river or spring water in the container and add the scent. Open the small jar of honey. Dip the middle finger of your left hand into the honey and *taste it first*! Then pour most of the honey into the scented water.

- Using your left hand, swirl the honey around in the scented water as you praise Oshun for Her intelligence, generosity, and beauty. Name the thing you wish to learn or the obstacle you want to overcome easily.

- Name the sacrifice you are willing to make to achieve the goal. Examples: "I'll study." "I'll save my money." "I'll forgive transgressions."

• When the feeling is right, dip your hands into the mixture and splash it on your body starting at your feet and *moving up* to the top of your head. Be sure to cover your navel, heart, throat, and third eye with the mixture. Pour the remaining mixture onto the very top of your head and rub it into your scalp. Be sure to anoint the temples and the back of your neck.

• Promise Oshun that you will be generous with the gift She bestows on you.

• Lightly dry your head and body with the towel.

• Wrap yourself in the fabric or skirt. Place the anklet of bells on your left ankle.

• Accept that your task will be easy to accomplish. Dance to a chosen piece of music (especially a song for Oshun) and accent the music by stomping your left foot.

The struggle is over. Let Her work the magic in your life.

Ose Otura

• "Ose Otura" is a very important story. To have Oshun leave us is a very dangerous thing! When Her departure appears on the divining tray, we look for its manifestation around us.

It's clear to see the effects of our behavior when we make Oshun angry. Many things bespeak the insult to Oshun, such as urban homelessness, the sexual abuse of children, and human trafficking. We must stop these things now and never let them happen again.

We also offend Oshun when we abuse our natural environment with, for example, commercial practices that harm bee populations. Bees, which are sacred to Oshun, are our most important pollinators. As they visit flora in their search for nectar, bees carry pollen from one blossom to another, allowing flowering plants to reproduce. Once the bees bring the nectar back to their hive, the colony transforms it into honey. But reckless agricultural practices have interfered with this cycle. Corporate bee farms have been replacing or supplementing these creatures' natural diets with white sugar, potentially weakening the antibacterial and anti-inflammatory effects of the bees' honey. Additionally, some beekeepers artificially inseminate queens, an act of rape that may have unforeseen consequences on social interactions within bee colonies. Habitat loss, pesticide use, pollution, and climate change all threaten to decimate populations of honeybees and other pollinators in various regions throughout the world. If we do not protect these ecologically essential creatures, our crops will fail, and many people will face famine.

In addition to protecting bees, in order to reconnect with Oshun, we must take better care of our water. Priests and shamans of every tradition, all over the world, are aware of its sacredness. And so we have been going to places where rivers are polluted or dry. We pick up trash and make offerings of honey, flowers, song, and prayer. We recognize the power of the divine feminine and beg Oshun to come back to us. To survive on this planet, we must become water defenders. You, too, can join the World Water Community at worldwatercommunity.com.

Ritual for Oshun's Forgiveness

You will need:

- A plastic bag

- A tool for picking up trash

- A jar of wildflower honey

- A packet of local wildflower seeds

- A bag of food to give away

Directions:

1. Find a source of sweet water, such as a river or stream.

2. Use your tools and bag to pick up any debris you encounter.

3. Open the jar of honey. **Always dip your finger in the honey and taste it.**

4. Pour the honey into the water.

5. Ask Oshun to forgive us for all manners of disrespect.

6. Collect some river water in the honey jar.

7. Whisper a prayer into the wildflower seeds, making a promise to honor the divine feminine.

8. Sprinkle the seeds along the banks of the river, leaving a trail of seeds as you exit the area.

9. On your way home, give food and water to the homeless and hungry people in your community.

10. Place the jar of honey water on your altar and use it to anoint your heart.

The Day Her Belly Burst

• Purchase a nice hand mirror. Decorate it with seashells, pearls, and silver beads. Set the mirror in a place where it can catch the light of the full moon. Gaze upon your own image and see the beauty of Yemaya reflected in your eyes.

• Contribute time, money, or both to a rape crisis center.

• Advocate on behalf of women's rights to control their own bodies.

• If you are a rape survivor, commit to your healing. Take a step now. Seek serenity by meditating before a large body of water.

Mother of the Night

• Consider the power and the importance of the women in your life. Write a poem to honor them.

Obatala's Mistake

• Are you a child of the first, sober making? Are you kind? Intelligent? Beautiful? Are you suffering from any malady of spirit? Addiction? Depression? Anxiety? Are you concerned about violence, hunger, environmental degradation? Appeals to Obatala/Iya Mapo can help.

Ebbo for Obatala's Aid

You will need:

> • A mat covered in white cloth
>
> • A small white saucer
>
> • A slip of white paper
>
> • A pencil

- White yam powder or cascarilla

- A clear glass

- Eight ounces of water

- A sheet of rolled cotton or cotton gauze

- A white candle (votive or tea light)

- Matches

Directions:

1. Sit quietly on the mat. Wear white clothing and cover your head. Meditate on the nature and details of your request.

2. Write your petition on the slip of paper, asking for the support you desire. Place the note inside the glass.

3. Sprinkle the white yam flour or cascarilla into the glass to cover the note.

4. Fill the glass with water. Sprinkle yam flour on the cotton. Cover the top of the glass with the cotton.

5. Place the saucer on top of the cotton. Be sure that the saucer is larger than the top of the glass and is flat against the surface. If a little cotton overlaps, do not worry. It will soak up moisture.

6. With your hand pressed against the saucer, *turn the glass upside down* so that the saucer is on the bottom, and the paper floats in the water.

7. Put the glass on your altar and place the candle on top of the glass. Light the candle and recite:

> *"May the Ancestors of all people*
> *Rise and awaken our minds.*
> *We ask for Protection for the people of the earth.*
> *We ask for the safety of All Life.*
> *We ask for the gifts of Clarity and Power,*
> *Courage and Humility,*
> *Abundance and Compassion,*
> *Intelligence and Beauty.*
>
> *We ask for all of Life's gifts in balance."*

8. If using a tea light or votive in a glass container, let the candle burn to completion. Seal the ritual with:

> *"It won't be long.*
> *It's not far away.*
> *We shall be seen in an abundance of blessings."*

9. You can refresh the candle as long as there is water in the glass. Continue to concentrate on the virtues you asked for. When the water evaporates, take the cotton and the paper to the top of a mountain or hill. Leave it on the branch of a tree.

The Coming of Iku

• What text(s) guides your understanding of death? The Bible? A Book of the Dead? Scientific information? Personal experiences?

• What is your attitude toward death? Fear? Anticipation? Sadness? Does this story change your attitude?

• Find a story from another culture that addresses the coming of death. How does that culture acknowledge death (rituals, festivals, etc.)?

The Oba's Feast

The story of "The Oba's Feast" provides us with three pieces of wisdom:

1. Beware of arrogance.
In our story, Obatala goes for divination to ask for guidance. Yet He allows His ego to override the very advice He came to seek. He chose not to make the sacrifice because He assumed that what He already knew was all that needed to be known. How different would the story be if Obatala had followed the directions of the Babalawo? Should the Babalawo have provided more information and insisted that Obatala make the offering?

Think of the times that you made a choice and had to take responsibility for the consequences of it. What is your definition of humility?

2. Respect the protocol of the culture.

Eventually, we come to understand that all the confusion—the imprisonment of Obatala, the disruption of the feast, and the loss of the community's respect—occurs because Elegba was not placated as the Babalawo recommended in the beginning. How would the story be different if Elegba had been invited to the feast? How do you respond to occurrences of "chance"?

3. Control the impact of the emotions.

Obba's primary identity is that of "the wife of Shango." She desires to gain favor with Shango and the guests by providing an exceptional soup. But the need for acceptance and recognition comes with a price that ultimately cost Her too much. Should She have been willing to sacrifice Her ear for the mushroom? What price are you willing to pay for social acceptance and emotional satisfaction?

Shango's temper allowed Him to start the feast without the presence of His father. This is a violation of the protocol. He exploded and cast Obba out unjustly without allowing a defense. Is this behavior befitting a political leader? What happens when rulers allow their own emotions to impact the conditions for the people?

Elegba commits the most outrageous act by engaging in a wrestling match with Iku, even after Obatala told Him that "no one can take life from Death." What happens when we attempt to manifest the impossible?

Acts to Honor Obba

• Create an altar for Obba. The altar should be laid on pink or purple cloth with candles of the same color. A bowl of river water and a plate of dried mushrooms should be placed in the center and surrounded by common items, such as a cooking implement, money earned in the market, a gele or crown, or a rock taken from a cemetery.

• Create an invocation acknowledging Her as the domestic goddess and the defender of abused women and ask for Her assistance in these areas of your concern.

• Learn about the healing power of mushrooms.

• Find a recipe and make a pot of wild mushroom soup. Then invite several couples to dinner.

• Make an offering of time or money to a women's domestic violence shelter.

Part II

The Division of the Cowries

• Visit your local flea or farmer's market. Bargain with the merchants there until you arrive at a fair price for the items you wish to buy. Then distribute these goods to the local homeless community.

• If you are dealing with a problem and can't seem to figure it out, gather a handful of popcorn kernels. Speak the concern into the popcorn and ask Elegba to "turn the trick in my favor." Find an intersection, a crossroads with four corners, near a bank, school, church, or hospital (any structure that represents the issue you are addressing). Walk into the middle of the intersection and toss the corn over your left shoulder. Thank Elegba, walk away, go home. Keep your eyes open, taking note of how things change. You'll be tricked into doing the right thing.

Elegba and the Two Friends

• The two friends argued over the colors of Elegba's hat, but they did not notice that He traveled in the same direction each time. Think of a time when you concentrated on one aspect of a problem only to discover that the real concern was something or someone else. What happened to change your perception of the problem? Did this shift lead to a different outcome or decision?

• Is your perception of reality defined by the thoughts and actions of your peer group? When something happens that allows you to "see things differently," how does this change your relationship to your peers? How do you handle standing in your own perception?

• When you must make important decisions, purchase an Elegba (red and black) candle for Him and place it near the entryway to your yard, porch, or home. Sit quietly and gaze upon the candle's light. Consider your options carefully. Ask for the "best life possible this lifetime." Decide and accept the consequences of your decision.

Ogun's Bush Knife

• If you experience a loss of employment, status, or respect due to conflicts between your material and emotional needs, you may feel that Ogun has abandoned you. To recall His power, you may dance in the forest (or local park) while you play agogô bells, beat pots and pans with a metal spoon, and brandish a machete. You can call Him back into your life.

• Learn something about an endangered animal species and contribute money to a wildlife preserve.

• Clean and sharpen the knives in your kitchen.

• Learn a craft such as jewelry making, wire sculpture, or forest foraging.

The First Grave

This story explains both the division of labor between men and women and the genesis of the burial customs of the Yoruba. In most societies, women are the carriers of culture, and men are the stewards of the material world. This is not true in every culture but was indeed true among the Yoruba and other West African people. Ask yourself these questions:

- How was the division of labor decided in your relationship, family, or household? Is it working? Does it utilize the talents of each party? Does it need improvement?

- What are the burial customs of your family, community, and culture? Does gender play into these customs, and if so, how? Are there ways you would reinvent the gendered aspects of these traditions?

- How important is the opinion of your community members to you? How does it impact your decisions and your life?

- Short of the kind of subterfuge Yemaya initially attempts, how do you go about making space for yourself, whether literal or metaphorical, within your day-to-day life and relationships? How could you do this differently?

Ochoosi's Arrow

• Take a walk in a nearby forest area. Walk carefully and quietly, trying not to trample the plants beneath your feet. As you walk, give thanks for the plants and animals living there. Practice due diligence in all your affairs and ask Ochoosi to guide you on your spiritual path.

• Guilt, grief, and shame are powerful emotions born of experiences that shake us to our very foundation. Post-traumatic stress disorder requires the assistance of a health care provider. If you have PTSD, please seek professional help. But the love of family and community is a major factor in recovery from trauma, too. Recovery is a time to forgive yourself and others, to release and let go, to slow down, breathe deeply, and accept support from the nature spirits.

• Practice walking on the earth with bare feet. Lie comfortably on a rock. Feel the sun on your skin and the wind in your hair.

• Retire early with a cup of soothing tea at night. Wake up in the morning to the songs of birds outside your window.

• Ask Ochoosi to give you the stealth of the tracker and the aim of the archer as you walk carefully on your spiritual path. Happy hunting.

The Deer Woman of Owo

In the nineties, I was conducting professional development workshops for women in leadership in corporations such as Charles Schwab, AT&T, and Pacific Bell. I employed this story in the process of mythosynthesis.[55] Each woman was invited to identify with a character in the story (based on her position in the workplace) and to act out the relationships as they existed in the present reality.

As you return to this story, consider identifying with each of the characters then shape-shift to see who or what you may become. This exercise could address a specific area of your life, such as work, or address your life and identity more broadly. Ask yourself these questions:

- Who am I?

- Who is the hunter? Who is the hunted?

- What needs are supported by whom? How?

- When and why did I accept my role in this story?

- How do I feel about the outcome of the story?

---

55   Mythosynthesis is a mode of growth and development therapy using the personal and social frame of reference that we call a myth. The mythosphere is the mythic envelope through which here-and-now experience is filtered. All human beings exist within their own mythosphere.

Back when I led these leadership workshops, after an in-depth discussion (which sometimes became an argument), participants were invited to "change the myth" to reflect their relational ideals. I invite you to do the same with your own myth.

The Legend of ObaKoso

Shango is invoked when we are faced with court cases and when we need the courage to stand up to oppression and lead the people to victory. He protects children and can perform great feats of magic.

Petition for Shango's Assistance

You will need:

- Six bright red apples

- Six red chili peppers

- Cotton balls

- A wooden bowl

- A red and white seven-day candle

- Honey

Directions:

1. Place the apples in the refrigerator to cool.

2. Wash the wooden bowl and line it with the cotton balls.

3. Rub your entire body with the six cool apples while reporting to Shango the injustices you have suffered.

4. Place the red and white seven-day candle in the center of the bowl.

5. Surround the candle with the six apples in the bowl and arrange the six whole red chili peppers between the apples.

6. Light the candle.

7. Cover the entire content of the bowl with honey.

8. Sit with this offering each day at the same hour. Remind Shango of His reputation as the greatest king of the powerful Oyo kingdom. Ask to be filled with courage. Ask to be surrounded by loyal and dedicated associates. Ask to be freed from excess egotism.

9. When the candle burns down, take this offering to the forest, leave it at the foot of a tree or under a bush, and feel confident that He will fight on your behalf.

The Calabash of Misfortune

Have you experienced the fulfillment of a prayer? Did you receive what you felt you deserved? How do you feel when a prayer goes unanswered?

Do you experience impatience? What are you most impatient about? What is the difference between impatience and "creative procrastination"?

To make good decisions, anoint your head.

You will need:

- A glass of water

- A candle

Directions:

1. Sit quietly with the candle and the clear glass of water.

2. Touch the top of the glass and draw a circle (clockwise) around the top of the glass. Then touch the glass at the four directions: north (12 o'clock), south (6 o'clock), east (3 o'clock), and west (9 o'clock).

3. Dip the longest finger on your left hand into the water at the middle of the intersecting point (the crossroad).

4. Anoint your third eye, the top of your head, and the back of your neck.

5. Say aloud, "My head supports me." Do this three times.

6. Sit quietly and think clearly.

Part III

The Mermaid's Lover

Indigenous cultures often have courtship rituals that support mate selection and marriage rites for creating families.

In modern society we have dating services to facilitate finding partners, civil procedures to protect shared property, and courts that regulate (or suppress) marriage rights.

But the power of attraction remains a mystery.

Who are you attracted to? What does attraction feel like?

Does your relationship require the approval of family, friends, coworkers, and neighbors?

Do you believe in marriage equality for all people?

Is your relationship threatened by law or societal disapproval? If so, what can you do about it?

Set a time to discuss issues of secrecy and transparency, boundaries and bonding, resource sharing, cultural differences, and spiritual beliefs—any subject that impacts the relationship.

Respect each other. Heal broken hearts. Grow and change together.

Remember to chant the magic words "I love you, I love you, I love you, I love you" as you go deeper together.

Olokun's Challenge

• This story acknowledges the creative power of the ocean, the force that gave birth to all life on Earth. Do you know what lies at the bottom of the ocean? What are the gifts humans receive from the sea?

• The tale also speaks to the dangers of violating that mysterious power. Do you know which human behaviors are damaging the ocean? What can you do about it?

Acts to Honor Yemaya-Olokun

You can perform any of these to bask in the power of the water spirits.

• Create an altar for Yemaya-Olokun. Choose a piece of blue and white cloth or one with an ocean theme. Upon it, place a white plate with a clear glass of water in the center. Surround the plate with shells, seaweed, driftwood, and other things from the ocean.

• Take a trip to the nearest body of water. Sit on the shore and contemplate the beauty of the water. Leave an offering of gratitude.

• Make a collage of your favorite sea creatures.

Olokun Rising:
A Praise-singing for the Waters of the World

This ritual was performed during the period of April 8–12, 2022. It can be replicated in a group or all alone. It is open to all people of all traditions, everywhere. It has four major components that can be performed by anyone, anytime. They are:

1. The Elevation of the Ancestors

- *Set an altar for the water spirits*: Please build an altar with photos and objects for the water deities, aquatic creatures, and wetlands. Make it powerful, beautiful, and safe.

- *Ancestors beneath the water*: Create a list of the ancestors who have died by water (e.g., during the Middle Passage, on pirate ships, during migration/ emigration, during floods/tsunamis/hurricanes, etc.).

- *Crystal bowl, bells, and candle meditation*: Place water and candles on the altar, ring bells, hum, cry, or moan, as your spirit guides. Relax, release, go inward. This may include a head cleansing.

2. An Educational Session

- Prepare and share an educational presentation on the conditions of the waters of the world. Select several YouTube videos, films, readings, and performances that explain the conditions of our waters and the impact of human behavior on them. Please tailor these recommendations to address your concerns. (In my ritual, people needed information on polar ice melting, tsunamis, fracking, and pollution.)

3. Journey to a Local Water Source

- Please go to the water source nearest you or travel to any body of water as directed by your ancestors and intuition. This could mean carpooling to a river, ocean, or lake or visiting a nearby location, like a park fountain, swimming pool, or even your kitchen sink.

4. Communion with the Water Spirits

- *Apology*: Apologize to the water spirits—on behalf of yourself, your family, your community, and the world—for wasting and polluting water. Ask for forgiveness.

- *A plea for salvation*: Whether in individual or collective prayer or song, express gratitude to the water spirits for their continued support of human life. Ask for the blessing you need and want. (In our ritual, we placed our apologies, our thanks, and our petitions onto the petals of flowers and threw them into the water. We sang a capella to Yemaya and Oshun, then had lunch at a roadside restaurant.)

- *Praise-singing the Water*: This could include:

  - Storytelling or dramatic reading

  - Drumming and dancing before the altar or playing small instruments

· Inviting people from different traditions to share stories about their water deities

• *Commitment to Sacred Waters*: Each person is asked to take an oath to protect and celebrate water.

This ritual was highly successful. Many people agreed that it should be an annual event. They agreed to organize regionally and to defend the water rights of Indigenous people.

Peace Nana

• To manifest alafia (good health and peace), I am asking every person to say a prayer in their own tradition asking for the end of human cruelty. Let the tendency to be cruel grow weaker in us. Pray it dissipates, melts, rolls down and out of our consciousness. Let us clean ourselves of the great diseases, fear and hatred. Then call upon the power to change ourselves on a cellular level and let us evolve into beings who are naturally compassionate.

• For guidance in prayers, see the anthology *Peace Prayers: Meditations, Affirmations, Invocations, Poems, and Prayers for Peace* (1992, Harper San Francisco).

The Wishing Star

The new moon is a time of increased optimism: the waters of the earth are increasing their influence on the land

and on the water in our bodies. During the new moon, we clarify our hopes, wishes, and expectations for the coming month.

Consulting a moon phase chart, watch the movement of the lights in the sky over the course of the month. When you see the star and crescent, gaze upon it and state your aspiration clearly as you point to the moon. Then take a deep breath, point to your heart, and visualize the wish granted.

During the next two weeks, commit some small act that moves you closer to your goal. Assess your progress on the next full moon.

Pouring Money Ritual

To raise your wealth thermostat, perform the money pouring ritual every new moon. You will manifest affluence (moving money like water), a natural increase in your material wealth, and personal satisfaction. This is to be done by an even number of people.

You will need:

- A strong desire to attract abundance

- The change from your pockets

- Two bowls of water

- A chant for wealth (see the following example)

• A green candle

• A rose of Jericho

• A symbol of wealth (ace of pentacles tarot card or a prosperity bill)

Directions:

1. Stand or sit in a circle.

2. Place your wealth symbol under, before, or beside your green candle. Light the candle.

3. Put all the change (coins) from your pockets into one bowl. Fill the bowl with water.

4. While reciting the chant for wealth, pour the bowl of money and water into the empty bowl held by the sister on your right.

5. Continue to pour the money from one bowl to the next, moving left to right, chanting until every woman has chanted at least eight times (the numeral eight is also the symbol for infinity).

6. Place the rose of Jericho in the bowl of water and watch the dry plant expand with life.

7. Place the bowl on the floor near the front door of the house where the ritual has been done.

Interesting things happen with this ritual. First, expect bitter arguments over money in the house. If respectfully handled, these arguments will expose budgetary excesses, wrong expenditures of energy, and dormant opportunities. This process is akin to the way the liver throws off poisons to clean the system. Those who have participated in the ritual find jobs for each other, create mutually lucrative ventures, and share the wealth of unexpected good fortune.

Important: Your wealth chant must be affirmative. Here is my favorite chant:

> "*Out of the Nowhere,*
> *Out of the Air,*
> *Out of the Darkness,*
> *To aid me, I swear*
> *Pile upon*
> *Pile of silver,*
> *Of gold,*
> *Come without warning*
>   *As you have been told.*"

IMAGE INDEX

Cowrie shell asterisks throughout text by Nedra Williams, 2022.

Page 23, KuroNekoNiyah, *Transatlantic Slave Trade Route*, 2021. CC BY-SA 4.0 <https://creativecommons.org/licenses/by-sa/4.0>, via Wikimedia Commons. Modified by Alex Dimeff.

Page 28, Nedra Willliams, *Dancing Women*. 2022.

Page 38, Nedra Williams, *As Above, So Below (2)*. 2022.

Page 48, Nedra Williams, *Oshun*. 2022.

Page 76, Nedra Williams, *Obba*. 2022.

Page 104, Gail Williams, *Marketplace 2*. 2022.

Page 126, Nedra Williams, *Oya*. 2022.

Page 132, Nedra Williams and Gail Williams, *Warriors*. 2022. (Ogun, Ochoosi, and cowries tray by Nedra Williams. Eshu Odara, iroko tree, and parrot by Gail Williams.)

Page 142, Gail Williams, *Shango Oba Koso 2 BW*. 2022.

Page 156, Gail Williams and Luisah Teish, *Oshun, Shango & Obatala*. 2022. (Oshun Ibukole by Luisah Teish, multimedia on canvas. Obatala, chameleon, cowries, tray with Eshu, spiral snake, Igba infinity, and Shango dancing by Gail Williams.)

Page 168, Carla Johnson and Nedra Williams, *Olokun*. 1992. (Olokun by Carla Johnson. Snake tray by Nedra Williams.)

Page 189, Nedra Williams, *Irosun Meji*. 2022.

ACKNOWLEDGEMENTS

Praise and thanks:

To my editor Chelsey Shannon, whose patience and support kept me going for years.

To Abram Himelstein for a sensible contract and the confidence in my ability to get the job done.

To Nedra Williams, Gail Williams, and Carla Johnson for the beautiful artwork that graces this book.

To my long-time friend and colleague Max Dashu for her profound work and a beautiful introduction.

To Alex Dimeff and their eye for color, shape, and sizing that made this book so attractive.

To Baba Obafemi of OIDSI and Baba Agboola, whose divinations refreshed my faith every time I faltered.

To the members of the Elegant Elders Council, who encouraged me on Monday afternoons to make it to Tuesday.

To the Jubilee Justice Committee (the J9) for confirming the importance of the ancestors' stories in our lives.

To my daughter Selana Lavonne, who made sure my social media worked as I slept.

To my hairdresser and makeup artist Zola Greer, who made sure that I looked my best all the time.

To all the people who encouraged me every day, especially the priests of Obba who brought the truth to light.